Dying a

A Dai and Julia Mystery

By E M Swift-Hook & Jane Jago

Dying as a Spy
by E M Swift-Hook & Jane Jago
ISBN: 9798768587963
Workingtitleblogspot@gmail.com
© 2021 Jane Jago & E M Swift-Hook

I

There were, Dai decided as his two children buried him in the sand on the beach at Traeth Abermaw for the third time that day, far worse times of year to be placed on gardening leave from his job as *Submagistratus* of *Demetae and Cornovii*.

It was not that he was under real suspicion, that had been made clear several times by the *Magistratus Domina* Agrippina Julius Valerius Apollinara, but the fact remained that Caeso Maol had been an acquaintance of his and he had not only been the one to find the body, but he had also been in the next room when the murder took place and so it was simply a matter of propriety and perception (her exact words) that Dai should be kept out of the gaze of both the public and officialdom whilst his wife Julia, who happened to be the other Submagistratus of Demetae and Cornovii, found out who had actually done it.

However, just because he was not involved in the investigation did not mean that, up to his neck in sand, arms behind his head, he could not spend some time considering it. The murder had taken place at an informal gathering of some of the well to do men of Viriconium. Dai had gone along as the guest of Paulus Vinicius Cato, a lawyer friend, who had virtually begged him to be there in order to make a gods-awful social commitment into something bearable.

"You can not imagine what these dos are like," Paulus had told him on the drive to the baths, "everyone trying to both show off how wonderful and independently successful they are and all at the same time trying to get the support of others for whatever their present pet project in self-promotion might be. I have to attend as half my clients go."

Dai could imagine, and had imagined, and had been close to making some careful social excuse to avoid the misery right at the last minute, but Paulus was a good friend and it was not a bad notion anyway for Dai to mix a bit with the kind of community that were attending.

They were almost exclusively Romano-British, with names that reflected the fact. Most had the defensive pride which many non-native Romans developed, seeing themselves one step up from their British neighbours, but never quite able to feel they were fully equal to a Roman citizen from *Italia* itself. And, to be fair, Dai knew that was not entirely their own fault. He, too, straddled that boundary and grappled with being seen as too Roman by the British and too British by the Romans. But he was fortunate in that his family was one that carried a lot of respect in the area and he had good friends in Rome, being married to a woman the *Praetor* regarded as a foster sister.

But for those without such advantages allowing them to maintain and deepen their connections in both directions, being Romano-British put them into an uncomfortable middle ground and, as a group, they tended to keep together.

That evening's gathering reflected a painful awareness of their cultural insecurity. It was held at the baths in Viriconium and then was to include a meal at *Aureum Anatisa*, the Golden Duck, a very expensive *caupona*, on the banks of the river. The Duck was one of less than a handful of exclusive *sub aquila* places in Viriconium, a building where the eagle above the entrance declared it was reserved exclusively for Citizens. But, ironically, the Duck was renowned for its excellent British menu. Dai had a feeling that the owners had cleverly, and cynically, carved their niche, by playing on the insecurities of these cross-culture families.

He had no opportunity to find out though, because whilst they were all having a post bathe massage before heading to the caupona, a scream from one of the staff had shattered his relaxation. The woman was screaming because there was blood trickling out from a changing cubicle and when Dai had pulled the door open, the body of Caeso Maol had literally fallen into his arms.

There would have been no suspicion of Dai at all had he not needed to use the urinal and left the main party for a few minutes shortly before the body was discovered. Which meant, in theory, he could have had time to kill poor Caeso. It did not help that earlier Caeso had been regalling the company as they sat in the hot room with tales from his schooldays—schooldays he had shared with Dai as they had happened to be in the same class—and not all the stories had been that complimentary to Dai, who had been a rather shy and studious nerd at that time.

So, expressing her profound regret at having to do so, the Magistratus had told Dai to take paid leave of absence and enjoy the summer sunshine and his children's company until the matter had been resolved.

He had decamped for the week to *Traeth Abermaw* taking his daughter, five year old Aelwen and her three year old brother, Rhodri together with their nursemaid, Luned and a discreet individual called Duggan—though whether that was his first or last name Dai was not entirely certain. The Magistratus had insisted on Duggan accompanying them to ensure their security. Dai had initially objected seeing no reason to have a bodyguard on a family holiday in the place where he himself had spent many happy such as a child, but Pina had simply knitted her brows and given him a stern look.

"Until we know what went on," she told him in a tone that was filled with the gravitas of her Imperial heritage, "we have no idea whether your being a witness might place you at an additional risk."

He could not argue that and to be fair to Duggan, the man was so little in evidence that Dai sometimes wondered if he had neglected his duty altogether and sloped off to the nearest *taberna*. So he was a bit surprised when he heard Luned say the man's name and opened his eyes to see the compactly muscular, steel eyed Duggan looking down at him.

"Someone named Cartival, dominus, says he knows you."

Dai tried to sit up, but the sand the children had packed firmly around him did not give way.

"Er—yes, that's Bryn," he said quickly, feeling acutely embarrassed to be stuck immobile in the sand. "Bryn Cartival is indeed a friend of mine. Thank you, Duggan."

The man gave a terse nod and Dai was sure there was a grin breaking out as he turned away, but perhaps that was just his own humiliation.

By the time Bryn had strolled over, carrying five dripping ice creams, Dai had managed to free himself from the beach, with the enthusiastic assistance of his two children and was dusting down the damp sand with a towel. Of course Bryn was the instant centre of attention and it was only once the ice creams had been distributed that he was able to escape from the excited children and a Luned who was trying very hard to make it clear that this was an exceptional treat, whilst licking the drips from her own cone with evident delight.

"I thought I better bring offerings," Bryn said as he held out the final, rather shapeless and melted ice cream to Dai. "They would have been less like libations if that security man had not insisted I waited at the top of the beach whilst he checked with you. There are these things called wristphones, you know. Most people have them." He nodded to where a pale band of skin around Dai's wrist stood testament to the absence of his own. Dai put his other hand over it self-consciously.

"I took it off to protect it from the sand and salt water," he lied. In fact it had been Luned insisting that if he was to spend the day on the beach with his children checking his wristphone every few minutes was a very poor example to be setting them. "So what brings you here? I'm sure it was not just the ice cream."

Bryn nodded and cast a glance towards where Luned and the two children were sitting on a striped picnic blanket with their half eaten cones.

"I was hoping I might be able to borrow you for the afternoon, that is, if you don't mind. Something's come up and as you are not working, I thought…"

Dai felt a sudden shift of gears deep in his psyche. He knew Bryn well enough to know he was not being asked to help follow a potential unfaithful spouse, which was the kind of work private investigators were supposed to make their bread and butter from.

"You thought?" Dai prompted.

"These robberies in the big villas—the ones you were just looking into when the mess with Moel happened? Well, they've made a few of the owners of bigger villas, mostly all citizens of course, very nervous and a few have asked me along to provide security consultancy, which I've been doing. You'd be shocked at how bad some of these places are. A teenager with a little initiative could break into most of them." He held up a hand as Dai opened his mouth. "Hear me out, Bard. Yes, I know you are on vacation here doing the quality-time thing, but I've been asked to do a security check on the villa owned by Mamercinus Aemilius Lepidus and he is in residence for the summer escaping the heat of Rome."

Dia gave a low whistle.

The Aemilii were one of the *gentes maiores*—the most patrician of patrician families who could trace their lineage back to year dot and claimed descent from the legendary second ever ruler of Rome after Romulus, Numa Pompilius.

He vaguely recalled being briefed by Caudinus soon after his arrival on the most important people who had residences in Demetae and Cornovii, but could not remember any mention of the name Aemilius.

"That must be a recent thing," he said, wondering how he could have missed it.

"Last month. A rapid purchase, from what I can gather. But when you are that kind of man you can buy a new villa in a day, I suppose."

"But why are you getting this job? Surely he will come fully provisioned with his own security team?"

"I am sure he does. But it seems like he wants some advice on local issues and someone suggested I was the man to provide that."

Dai nodded, seeing now where this was going.

"And having the local submagistratus along, complete with ring of citizenship is going to ensure you a better reception than just arriving to criticise his expensive and expansive security arrangements and will soften the blow when you have to tell him why his Roman methods might not be so effective in darkest *Britannia*?"

Bryn sighed and gave a lop-sided grin.

"Something like that," he agreed.

"So where is this villa?"

"Just outside *Penllwyn*, on the banks of Afon Melindwr. Not far at all. We could be there and back in an afternoon."

"The only problem I see with your plan," Dai said, holding up his index finger with its ring, "is that one of the gentes maiores is not likely to be very impressed by a silver band of citizenship. They likely look down on most native born Romans, so might be completely dismissive of a provincial oick who somehow got granted citizenship."

Bryn's grin broadened because he surely knew by then that Dai was going to agree.

"Then it'll be just like the old days then, won't it?"

***

It had been rather earlier in the morning than Julia really wanted to be on the road, but a summons to a meeting with the Magistratus was more or less an imperial decree. *Ientaculum* meetings were apparently all the fashion in Rome right now, so Julia was dressed smartly and bowling along the imperial highway towards *Viriconium* before her eyes were truly open. Her Senior Investigator who also happened to be her husband's *vitricus*, Gaius Brutus Gallus, cracked his jaw in an enormous yawn.

"The devil fly away with the woman," he grumbled. "What maggot has got into her brain now?"

Edbert answered from the driving seat. "It's her fancy imperial cousin who is staying with her. Keeps dropping the latest fashions in Rome into the conversation. Bedwyr thinks the woman is taking the *mingo*."

Julia sighed. "Well I'm going to have a word. Agrippina may be my boss, but she has to realise she's currently down a submagistratus."

"And that means you don't have the time to be popping along to Viriconium just to smooth her ego." Edbert had the right of it, of course, but putting it that bluntly made Julia wince.

"Why does Bedwyr think the mingo is being extracted?"

"Because he can see the imperial cousin laughing behind her hand, and so can Domina Annia, but Domina Agrippina is in one of her moods."

"Which one?"

"Overbearingly gracious."

"Oh that one. We had some experience of that when she believed Bestia's lies about Dai. Why is she like it now?"

"Bedwyr says she don't much like her cousin. But feels obliged to offer sanctuary as the woman is disabled. Ski-ing accident apparently."

Julia sighed. "This could be all sorts of awkward, then."

"It could. If you let it. Time to poker up and do your best Domina Julia face."

Julia made a very rude noise. "I suppose that explains why Viriconium, not Annia's villa. Which is a site closer."

"Indeed. But so much less formal."

Gallus grunted. "I think I'd be better off going to the kitchen with Edbert."

Julia showed him her teeth. "You don't get away that lightly. If the Magistratus wants an ientaculum meeting that's what she's going to get. And if I'd any forethought I'd have brought Angie Ffrydd along too."

There being not much more to say, the rest of the journey was completed in silence, with Gallus going so far as to close his eyes and pass the time dozing gently.

At the portico of the Magistratus' official dwelling, a uniformed porter leapt forward to open the door of the all-wheel. Julia snarled at him and he refrained from attempting to help her out of the vehicle.

With Gallus at her shoulder she turned to look at Edbert. "I'll buzz you when I'm ready to leave."

"Yes Domina Julia." His voice was the perfect blend of respect and polite blandness, but his eyes were alight with unholy amusement. Julia offered him the suspicion of a wink before following the porter into the building.

The Magistratus, her partner Annia, and a thin brown-skinned woman who leaned heavily on a single elbow crutch were just arriving in the *atrium*.

"Ah, Julia, on time as ever. And you have brought along your Senior Investigator…"

The Magistratus was obviously struggling over what to say next, and Julia let her fumble for a few seconds before speaking briskly.

"You said 'meeting'. And SI Gallus always accompanies me to meetings."

This being inalienable, Agrippina led the way into the garden, where a simple buffet meal was laid out. Julia was glad to see chairs around a white-clothed table as the idea of sharing a *lectus* with any of the others was unappealing.

Annia caught her eye and made a deprecating face to which Julia replied with a grin.

They filled their plates and sat down to 'enjoy' what Julia thought was probably the most awkward meal it had ever been her misfortune to sit through. Pina was at her Imperial worst, Annia stared at her plate and refused to meet anybody's eyes, Gallus ate in stoic silence, and the visitor, who was introduced as 'Ancilla', made small talk in a patrician drawl. It didn't take long to hear the undertones of belittlement and not-so-subtle mockery of anything and anyone attached to the Magistratus. Julia gritted her teeth, and made a mental note to leave as soon as common civility permitted. She could, she thought, survive without blowing a steam valve if she just concentrated on her food and let the flood of petty malice flow over and around her without actually listening.

She was doing pretty well until the plates were cleared, when Ancilla addressed her directly.

"Now, Julia *parva*, do tell us all about the sheep stealing and tractor rustling that passes for crime in this armpit of the Empire."

Julia raised her face and looked straight into the eyes of her would-be tormentor. She waited a beat then raised one eyebrow. Ancilla snorted and stared down her patrician nose. Julia, who had grown up in the slums around the skirts of Rome, wasn't one whit abashed by the older woman's stare.

Seeing that Julia wasn't impressed, Ancilla tried another tack. She turned her face to Pina.

"I thought we were here for a meeting. When will it convene?"

"As soon as you and Domina Annia leave." Julia saved her boss the bother of a reply.

For a moment, Ancilla's reaction hung in the balance. Then she painted on a smile.

"*Mea culpa*," she said, adding a bright, tinkling laugh. "You are, of course, correct. My own frustration at the limitations of my body, and the dreariness of constant pain caused me to overstep the mark. Please excuse me."

Julia was not to be so easily mollified and she looked steadily into the bright, malicious eyes. Ancilla put up with this for a few seconds before hunching a pettish shoulder.

"What is one to do, except amuse oneself where one can?"

"Perhaps you should speak to a *medicus* with experience of pain control. I believe there is one such with a province wide reputation at the *asclepieion* on *Ynys Mon*. As for the rest, you might consider not venting your spleen on those around you. None of whom was the architect of your misfortune."

You could have cut the tension around the table with a very blunt knife and Julia felt Gallus draw himself together in case action was necessary. In the event, though, it was all a bit of an anticlimax.

Ancilla gave a shout of what sounded like genuine amusement and spoke in a completely different voice from the light, malicious drawl that had had Julia itching to box her ears.

"Busted. I really have been behaving like a spoilt brat."

Julia wisely forbore from comment.

Pina took up the conversational baton.

"Perhaps we could convene in my office."

She led the way with Julia and Gallus at her heels. Once inside the quiet room, Pina so far forgot her imperial dignity as to laugh until she cried. Julia watched patiently and when her boss recovered shook her head.

"I have to say 1 am delighted at the way you outed Ancilla. She is by way of a distant relative and our mothers were close so we were often together as children, but I have to say we've grown apart long since. We've barely spoken since childhood. I could not refuse her, though, when she asked to come and stay. I helped her son get an administrative job in the area some time ago and she wanted to visit him and thank me in person. But I have to say she has been pretty dreadful since she arrived."

Julia grinned. "Happy to be of assistance," she said and gave a military style salute. "Permission to return to work, domina."

"Yes. Off you go. And, Julia. Thank you."

Julia and Gallus made good their escape.

If she had thought the day was going to improve after that, Julia would have been disappointed. Although, in all truth, she hadn't expected it to get much better, she hadn't expected it to get so much worse.

She gritted her teeth and resisted the temptation to kick the ample buttocks of the insurance assessor who had been awaiting her and Gallus on their return, preventing them from getting on with the work in hand and who was now lecturing-stroke-hectoring her about the amounts of money his employers were losing in the spate of jewellery robberies the *Vigiles* were currently investigating.

Annoying though his peroration was, it was clear to Julia's experienced eye that this was merely by way of a diversion before he came to his main point—whatever that might be. A shift in his stance and the out-thrusting of his many chins gave notice that he was at last coming to the point of his visit.

"It's obvious," he said portentously, "to the experienced investigator that the local so-called law enforcement must be involved in the robberies."

Julia bit hard on her anger. This was Angharad Ffridd's case, Dai's SI, and she had been running it very professionally.

"And this would be because?" Anyone who knew Julia would have taken the extreme sweetness of her tones as a warning to take cover, but the fat functionary kept right on digging his own grave.

"This would be because there must be a blind eye being turned."

"And you think this because…" Julia let the sentence drift.

"Because there is no other possible explanation, and I'm sure if your husband was in charge of this investigation."

The icy quality of the silence that followed this remark brought hectic colour to the man's cheeks, but he was obviously not about to be faced down by a small woman and he harrumphed like a stranded walrus.

"The thing is," Julia spoke in her most honeyed tones, "there's quite a list of people who have recently had 'business' with the burgled villas. Your own name is quite high on that list."

"Insolence. I will not be accused by some slip of a girl."

"It isn't *I* who am insolent."

He reared back as if slapped. "You might not care for such plain speaking, Domina Julia, but the fact remains that Dominus Llewellyn is the most senior Vigiles hereabouts."

"Because he is a man?"

Finally, Julia's visitor realised that he had talked himself into an awkward corner and he fell silent.

Gallus laughed. It was a short humourless bark of sound.

"Shall I see the dominus to his vehicle?"

"In a moment." Julia turned a basilisk stare on the fidgeting figure. "For your information, there is a list of about twenty people who are currently under investigation. I'm sure an officer will be visiting you soon. And now I bid you good day."

Gallus wheeled the gobbling man out of the room before he could try Julia's patience any further. When he returned, Gallus showed his excellent teeth in a wolfish grin.

"I think," he said cheerfully, "your erstwhile guest may have made *merda* in his underwear."

"Why would that be? He obviously wasn't scared by me."

"No. So I put the fear of gods in him for you."

18

Julia was immeasurably cheered by his support, even if it wasn't good politics to say so.

"What did he seek to accomplish by coming here and annoying me?"

"I think he meant to intimidate rather than irritate."

"Wanting to turn the spotlight firmly onto the Vigiles?"

"Yes. I get the impression that somebody leaned on him and sent him to lean on you. Which at least lets us know that whoever is behind him really doesn't know you."

Julia's smile was vicious. "Not even by reputation I would think. However, it isn't even our case, it's firmly in Angie Ffridd's lap, because, when it comes to a short-staffed department, murder trumps robbery even if the dead gentleman doesn't seem to have been a pattern card of probity and virtue."

"No indeed. There does appear to be quite a list of people who might have had reason to dispose of him."

"Or have him disposed of."

"For now, will you reach out to Angie and ask her to pay special attention to our visitor."

"Shouldn't you be doing that?"

"Umm…" Julia felt herself blushing

"If Bryn was still Dai's SI you'd have no problem telling him."

"No. But…"

"No buts. She's a decent human being and very good at her job. And she doesn't even have the hots for Dai any more. He has to learn to trust her and you have to stop seeing her through his eyes."

The rebuke was mild enough, but Gallus didn't often take Julia to task, so when he did she listened. She had a quick think and had to confess that she wasn't being fair to a woman who was indeed proving an asset to the vigiles.

"Yes. I'm being stupid. I'll speak to her at once."

Gallus laughed. "I can do it, and it's probably easier if I do as we speak often. I just needed you to have a look at how you and Dai are being with Angie."

"Yes. Point taken. I'll have a word with Dai as well. Better still I'll set Caudinus on him, when he and Cariad and the family arrive for their summer visit."

Gallus grinned. "Good tactics *filia mea.* A word from the man he loves like a father might just turn the trick."

Julia looked at his square, dependable face. "You don't mind that your stepson loves another man like a father?"

"Why would I? Dai and I didn't get off to the best start so I'm glad we have become friends. Wanting more would be greed, as this place has already given me a life I never dreamed of." He flicked Julia on the end of her nose and went away moving with quiet purpose.

Julia was up to her knees in paperwork when he returned.

"What's all that?"

"It's the overtime and expenses chits that Dai appears to have overlooked for the past six months."

"Angie does that for him. Says she initialled a batch only yesterday."

Julia looked at the papers. "There's no initials here. I think somebody is trying to take advantage of the lack of a second Submagistratus to pull a fast one."

"I wouldn't be surprised. Give me the papers and I'll make some calls. Help Angie put the fear of her wrath into a few greedy clerks."

"Please do. I'm sure Dai would do the same thing."

"He would, and we could do with him being back at work. But I'm sure he and the offspring are having a wonderful time at Abermaw. The weather is just right for a seaside holiday."

Julia punched him lightly on the biceps. "Stop winding me up, will you?" She felt the little knot of sadness in her chest loosen, and understood that had been his aim. She smiled into his broad, strong face. "I was never going to be able to go with them, was I?"

"No filia mia. As long as you two represent the rule of law hereabouts at least one of you has to be here at all times."

"We chose our path. I just miss them all."

As they were alone, Gallus pulled her into a wholly unprofessional hug. "Shouldn't be for long. If it's any consolation, Olwen is making my life a misery because she is missing them and because she thinks fingers are being pointed at Dai."

Being very aware of how her mother-in-law could be, Julia winced on Gallus' behalf.

"Why don't you send her to Abermaw on a visit?"

"Because Dai made me promise not to. Apparently Luned has sworn to resign if Olwen appears without somebody to keep her fingers out of the child-rearing pie."

"A tap on the door had Gallus stepping back a pace.

"Come in," Julia called.

The quietly efficient secretarius Paulus had found for her came into the room. "The post mortem report on Caeso Maol is in, Domina Julia. And the Praetor begs the favour of a word."

Julia laughed. "I bet he didn't use those words Osian."

"I wasn't privy to his words, Domina, one of his secretaries called me."

"Okay, leave the post mortem report here. And patch the Praetor straight through as soon as he calls."

"Yes Domina."

Osian went out and closed the door quietly behind him.

"That's a very good lad," Gallus remarked. "But how in the name of Hades are you supposed to say his name?"

"Osheen, like I just did."

Gallus balked slightly. "Are you sure?"

"I am. I asked his mam."

Julia dropped the PM report she had been scanning as she spoke. "That's a lot of use. Tells us our deader was stabbed. Although the useless *spado* has at least sent off some samples for a toxicology report."

Gallus picked up the single page and grunted noncommittally.

At that precise second, Julia's desktop unit bleeped and the *Praetor* of Rome's impressively aquiline features filled the screen.

"Are you alone?"

"Hello Hook-Beak. Gallus is here."

"Hello yourself. But no time for niceties. Gallus is as close-mouthed as an oyster so he can stay."

"Stay for what?"

"We may have a problem…"

Julia glared at the image of the man she regarded as a brother.

"Which we is this? Rome or here?"

Hook-Beak snorted. "How about both?"

"Both?"

"Yup. As you know, I keep a paternal eye on the law enforcement side of things."

Julia's mind slid over the idea of her childhood friend as paternal—he had always been ruthless and abrasive and the murder of his wife had made him about as cuddly as steel wool—but she nodded obligingly.

He showed his teeth in a feral grin. "Be that as it may. My paternal eye has been caught by the odd movements of some undesirable sorts I can only call *praecipuum ponebaturs*. I hate those people, little better than professional killers but with the sheen of legality as they are after criminals and only get paid by results. It looks as though something—or someone—in Britannia is drawing their attention. I have people looking into what that might be but so far I have heard nothing and have no idea what is going on there."

"Me neither. Have the people under your paternal eye come up with any clues?"

"Not that they are telling me about. But I think there's something. I'm digging." He lifted his heavily muscled shoulders and grimaced.

Julia felt a brief pang of pity for anyone who got in his way, but she read something more than annoyance in the back of his hooded eyes.

"Okay spado. What are you not telling me?"

He sighed.

"The very worst of the praecipuum ponebaturs are circling like vultures, which was only to be expected. But. We've lost sight of a couple of the nastiest *irrumators*, last seen heading for Britannia and I'm afraid the first we might know about where they are is when a body turns up. I've alerted *Londinium* and I'll send you their details too so you know who to look out for."

Julia swore briefly. "The last thing we need is those *fui draconii* sniffing around."

Gallus grunted. "I'll just send a message to Abermaw, shall I?"

"Who is in Abermaw?" Hook-Beak demanded.

"Dai and the children. He's on gardening leave. Wrong place, wrong time. Found a body."

Hook-Beak nodded just once. "Yes. He needs to know who might be on the ground. If I learn any more I'll get right back to you."

Then he was gone. As abruptly as ever.

Julia stared at the darkening screen for a moment. "Who do we need to tell, Gallus?"

"Aside from Dai. Bryn, and Edbert? The Magistratus, your secretarius and Angie. No need for any more right now."

Julia nodded. "I should meet with Angie shouldn't I."

"If you want to build a bridge."

"I do."

"That's my girl."

When Gallus had gone about his business, Julia thought about the insights and emotions he was in the habit of hiding under his granite exterior and felt quite small and humble. She and Dai had rather dismissed Angie as a silly girl with her head full of romance, but Gallus had easily made her understand that was both lazy and unkind. She vowed to do better.

For now, though, she had work, and a conversation with her boss who may or may not be pleased to know what was afoot. But at least Julia had the pleasant anticipation of tomorrow's visit from Dai's sister, Cariad, who lived in much warmer climes for the health of her husband and seldom visited but had become one of Julia's closest female friends. She buzzed Osian who arrived promptly.

"We may have a bit of a security problem right now. I want you to…"

Julia noticed he was blushing.

"Have you been eavesdropping?"

He nodded miserably.

"Why?"

"Because that's the usual way my kind keeps abreast of what the boss needs. It's normally the only way to avoid being yelled at."

"Not here, though."

"No. But the habit is ingrained."

Julia shook her head. "What about if I specifically told you not to listen to something?"

"I wouldn't listen." He said, and his simplicity was far more convincing that a theatrical vow would have been.

"Very well then. You know why you need to be careful right now."

"I do domina."

He turned to go, and as his hand touched the door Julia spoke quietly.

"Osian. It really wouldn't be a good idea to betray my trust."

He turned and flashed her a wide smile.

"Oh. I know that right enough. If your SI left any of me to stomp, Edbert would stomp it and feed the resulting soup to a pack of small, ugly dogs."

Julia laughed. "So long as you know."

He sobered. "I do. But the reason I'd never betray you is to do with you, not them."

Julia watched his disappearing back and wondered why he would think she was deserving of his loyalty. Deciding she didn't know, she buzzed Edbert. The man mountain appeared with his usual swiftness.

"You rang, domina?"

"I did. According to Hook-Beak we could have a couple of praecipuum ponebaturs on our patch. Target unknown."

Edbert cracked his knuckles, which made a noise like a gunshot.

"Don't do that, spado. It's annoying."

"I know. But it relieves my feelings. Does Dai know?"

"Gallus is sending him a message."

"That'll be crisp and to the point then."

"And it wouldn't if I let you go and see him?"

"Oh it would. I just fancied a swim."

Julia chuckled. "Well you aren't going to get one." She sighed. "I'm going to have to put Angie Ffridd in the picture, and I'm not looking forward to that conversation."

"Why not? She's all right. And anyway it's about time you give the poor silly *moecha* a chance. She can't help it if Dai makes her heart go pitty-pat. He has that effect on a lot of people, you know."

"Yes. I do know. But not, until recently, his SI."

Edbert nodded and pushed out his lower lip as if considering that seriously. "Dai doesn't swing that way and neither does Bryn. But Bedwyr admits to the odd erotic fantasy about his manly frame."

Julia didn't know whether to giggle or be appalled so she temporised by stretching her eyes and smiling demurely.

Edbert's grin was unrepentantly reminiscent and Julia clapped her hands over her ears.

"Do. Not. Tell. Me."

"Oh. I wasn't going to. I'll just take a walk around household security, shall I? I'm sure Gallus is ahead of me, but it won't do any harm to emphasise the point."

"It won't indeed. Will you send Osian in please."

He patted her arm with a huge hand and ambled off. Osian came in with his usual quiet step.

"How may I assist you, domina?"

"Can you get hold of Angie Ffridd at headquarters and ask her to come and see me, please?"

He nodded and disappeared.disappeared, returning five minutes later.

"I have located Angharad Ffridd. When do you require her presence?"

Julia looked at the time.

"Will you ask her if she would like to come and eat *cinio* with me?"

"Ask?"

"Yes. Angie is Dai's SI and should be treated with respect."

Osian looked puzzled and Julia raised one eyebrow.

"I thought Bryn Cartivel was Dominus Llewellyn's SI."

"He used to be. But he's retired now. Angie is his replacement." Julia decided frankness was called for. "It may not be running too smoothly yet. And Dai's gardening leave isn't helping."

"I see. Although I feel that I should have known the situation."

Julia smiled at him. "I don't see how you can be expected to know everything, particularly as I have a special dispensation to work from here instead of the offices in Viriconium."

"Even so…"

"Stop beating yourself up and invite the girl to eat cinio with me. You too if you would like, it would be helpful if you got to know her a little. Tell her I can promise a good meal and some Llewellyn Red."

"What time?"

"Six thirty."

He went about his business and Julia bunked off work for a quick visit to Cookie.

II

Dai left Luned to take the children to an indoor play park with slides, crawl ways and ball pools—and a fast food *popina* which served all the things the children were never allowed to eat at home. He trusted Luned to let them enjoy that treat without overindulging. Duggan accepted his instruction to remain with the children, but his appraising gaze assessed Bryn before he gave a terse nod, leaving Dai with the distinct impression that had he disapproved of Bryn as a potential security guard, he would have dug in his heels over the idea.

Dai decided to take his hovercar, which managed the narrow and often unmetalled roads slightly less well than Bryn's decent all-wheeler, but would impress upon arrival much more than that battered vehicle. They were already on the road when Gallus called with news that the Praetor was concerned that some professional hunters of criminals were operating in Britannia. Dai found that news disturbing on two levels—both that it meant such dangerous and disreputable people were on the loose and their whereabouts unknown and that if they were here then it meant a major criminal was also likely to be operating beneath the radar. He took some small comfort from the almost certain assurance that whoever they were after would be in Londinium and extremely unlikely to trouble them in Viriconium.

The villa at Penllwyn, Dai decided, was more than impressive.

Rising three stories in places, with arms enclosing a courtyard with fountains and statuary and broad pleasure gardens reaching down to the river. It sat on a low hill, embraced in the verdant green for which Britannia was so rightly famed across the Empire. A temperate delight which drew men like Mamercinus Aemilius Lepidus from the parched Roman countryside to enjoy a summer of more convivial heat and without the kind of insects that might bite. Although for many the price for that in terms of being away from Rome for even a moment, was higher than they were willing to pay. Factional conflicts meant presence at the heart of the Empire an existential essential for some.

But perhaps Aemilus was not of that kind. Perhaps his distinction and the antiquity of his family made him one more often sought out than seeking patronage. Dai tried to keep himself distant from such things, even whilst being painfully aware that his own family's fortunes were tied to one such faction and that they could rise and fall with them.

Close to, they were stopped at a security gate and the guard, who looked to Dai to be a retired praetorian special ops veteran at the very least, took his time checking their ID, but did have the grace to offer Dai a stiff salute once his rank was established.

"Did you see that?" Bryn murmured as they eased their way along the driveway which was lined with poplar trees.

"Nerve whip?"

Bryn nodded his expression a little grim.

In theory the nerve whip saved lives. It was a non-lethal weapon which any and every Roman citizen was free to carry and to use on non-citizens who they felt threatened them. In big provincial capitals like Londinium, it was a very usual thing to see as threats from street criminals were high. And in such a setting, Dai acknowledged, it was likely better than having every citizen lethally armed.

But in Viriconium the only people who even thought of wearing a nerve-whip were those who were the prejudiced and bigoted kind. In fact, seeing someone wearing one was something Dai always took as a sign that he was not going to get along with them. He was not alone in that. Every non-citizen in the Empire, even those who were happily acclimatised to Roman rule, saw the nerve-whip as a symbol of Roman oppression. And most Romans, as Dai well knew, were very aware of that and avoided carrying one—openly at least—for that very reason.

"Old habits, perhaps?" Dai suggested.

"It won't make them any friends around here."

"Perhaps they are not interested in making friends. I have a feeling this is more a man set on keeping himself to himself. Remind me to check that the Magistratus knows he is living here."

It was not the most promising of starts to their visit and when they reached the house it was to find the drive that led to the front was blocked by a chained bar and they had to drive past and to the rear of the building.

"Tradesman's entrance," Bryn said. "It gets better and better."

"There was an eagle over the main entrance," Dai observed, sourly. "Old school patricians of the worst kind."

It did not always work that way. The Magistratus was of the most noble blood any patrician could be—that of the Divine Diocletian himself—and yet for all her flaws, she was as far from the nerve-whip wielding, sub aquila insisting, stereotypical patrician as one could imagine.

They parked up in a potholed carpark at the back of the house, beside a row of wheelie bins and a pungent compost heap. Stepping carefully to avoid the puddles and mud, Dai wondered if perhaps he should have donned a *toga* for the visit, just to make a point.

Halfway to the door, it opened and a tall woman in her late teens or early twenties emerged, clad in designer garb and with her luxuriant black hair coiled into a complex coiffure that Dai guessed was going to be the latest fashion in Rome. She took a few steps towards them then stopped, her expression a fixed smile. The image of a young and novice hostess caught in a social dilemma.

"Submagistratus Llewellyn?"

Dai closed the remaining distance between them, aware that Bryn was giving him space to make the first encounter.

"I am so sorry," the woman went on, "the man on the gate was slow telling us of your arrival or I would have lifted the barrier to the portico."

"That's alright," Dai said quickly, "we would have had to come in this door anyway." He made a slight gesture towards Bryn.

Her face fell. "Oh no, it's not…" The colour rose in her cheeks. "My father insists on tradition, you see." Then she held out a hand. "Aemilia Aemilius Secunda. I am here to oversee the household for my father as he is presently unmarried." She barely touched Dai's fingers before turning to Bryn. "You must be the local security consultant? We have been expecting you and my father has set everything out that you might need to see. If you would both come with me."

That the daughter of the house herself had thought it needful to welcome them did much in Dai's view to ameliorate the previous impression he had held of the household. But meeting her father restored it all again and with extra force.

The room they were shown to was lavishly furnished, if in a typically Britannian style and reflected little of the chilling Roman minimalism of its owner. Dai half suspected that the villa must have been purchased pre-furnished, and made a mental note to find out if that was indeed so.

Aemilius himself was a granite jawed, gimlet eyed man in his early fifties. His hair had taken on a steel grey as if in tribute to his nature. He wore the toga-styled tunic and trews, which was increasingly favoured as smart casual wear in the most Roman of circles and—to Dai's delight—was even becoming accepted for light formal wear too in place of the cumbersome true toga. He responded to the introductions with a brief uplift of his chin and then gestured to the table beside him where there was an open laptop and sheets of paper laid out.

"Plans. Schemata etc. etc. Any questions. Ask."

"Could we speak to your head of security, please dominus?" Bryn asked.

For a moment Aemilius frowned, as if he resented being directly addressed by a non-citizen. A look Dai knew so well from his years in Londinium.

"You are," he said and snapped his jaw closed, glaring at them with something close to defiance.

Bryn sloped his shoulders and gestured to the table.

"Then perhaps you could talk us through what you have here, dominus. It would save a lot of time if—"

"Whose time?" Aemilius demanded "You are the expert. You are paid for this. You do the work."

Byrn rocked back on his heels and Dai saw the brief flash of anger illuminate his eyes, gone before it could take root. A lifetime of bad tempered patricians had imured him to such provocation.

"As you wish, dominus, but if you wish to benefit fully from the local element I can bring to your overall security, it would be extremely helpful for me to understand your present take on it."

His daughter had been standing back, but now stepped forward, her face pale.

"Father, you know the security here so well, it would take you no time at all to explain it."

Aemilius' demeanour changed almost instantly. Like a bristling war hound gentled, he gave his daughter a look which seemed a little odd to Dai and then nodded. Dai had a sudden flash of insight which showed her being frequently thrust into the role of mediator.

The actual consultation took less time than Dai had imagined it might. For all his extreme arrogance and short temper Aemilius seemed very well informed on state of the art security measures and surprisingly unresistant to the suggestions Bryn—and Dai himself—came up with for improving them to meet local conditions.

They were almost done when Aemilius' wristphone beeped and he glanced at it then turned and strode to the door. As he opened it he turned and gave a curt nod.

"Send your report by tomorrow *prandium*. Aemilia will see you out."

She did. The way they had come in.

"I apologise for my father. This security check-up was at my insistence, he only agreed because I said I did not feel completely safe. He was a prisoner of war in the Mongol Empire for nearly twelve years and was only freed a couple of months ago. He returned to Rome to find our affairs in ruins, his wife remarried and his only son dead in a border skirmish." She stopped and spread her hands against the silk of her *stola*. "I am all he has left. He could not bear to remain in Rome so we came here. "

"I am sorry to hear of it, domina," Dai said, sincerely. "But what of your older sister?"

She gave him a thin smile.

"There never was a Prima, I was the second child not the second daughter," she explained. "My father never had much imagination. My half-brother was called Primus."

The conversation took them to the door, where she bade them farewell and thanked them, standing on the step until Dai lost sight of her in his rearview mirror as he drove around the corner of the villa.

"Strange set up," he said once they were free of the villa grounds and back on the road to Abermaw. "Did you notice there were very few household servants in evidence? though for such a large place there must be a decent sized staff."

"You would think that," Bryn agreed, "and I'll tell you something even more odd—the security system there is as much about inside the house as outside it. He was focusing on the external stuff, but I took a look at the rest whilst you were talking about local anti-Roman sentiment and that house is wired in almost every room."

Dai thought about that and felt his brow crease.

"He watches the whole house?"

"If he does it's not from that laptop. There was no access to the system on it at all." Then Bryn sighed. "I am making a mystery out of nothing. The man clearly has some kind of post traumatic issues and is probably paranoid enough as a result to want to be able to check on his staff at any time."

"Maybe that's why he seems to have so few. But once you've got that report written it is not your problem." Dai's stomach rumbled and he realised he had missed prandium. "Will you stay to eat? Or are you heading back right?"

And the conversation turned to other things.

***

After an afternoon investigating the murky finances of the murdered man she had mentally labelled Moley, Julia was more than ready for food and a big glass of wine. She was less enthusiastic about her guest, but gave herself a firm talking to as she washed her hands and face. Angie was someone who was doing her best and needed to be made an ally for everyone's sake.

She went into the summer atrium, where her housekeeper, Elfrida, had laid a very pretty informal table and there was an opened bottle of Llewellyn Red breathing. It was a very fine wine made from the produce of vineyards owned by Dai's older brother, although Llewellyn was a name more renowned for its brandy. Pouring herself a big glass she moved to the glass wall that had been rolled open to allow the scents of the garden into the room. The garden was quiet and Julia felt a pang of loneliness as she missed the clamour of children's voices. The sound of toenails on the marble floor alerted her to the arrival of her little white sleeve dog. She bent down and smoothed the silky fur.

"Hello Merch. Have you come to keep me company?"

"She has indeed." Edbert laughed. "And here come the boys."

Four wolfhounds piled into the room and greeted their mistress with great enthusiasm. Huginn and Muninn were younger and faster, but they stood back while Canis and Lupo spoke to Julia, coming for their ear scratches with commendable gentleness when it was their turn.

"These two are proper gentlemen now."

Edbert snorted. "Not when there's food about."

Julia stood with a hand on each black head. "They're only babies."

"You always defend those you love, don't you?"

"Of course I do. That's what love is all about."

"Yes. It is, even if the recipient is undeserving."

Julia heard a certain hardening in his deep tones. "Spit it out, man. Who is undeserving."

"Bedwyr's *cunnus* of a baby brother," Edbert all but growled.

"I never knew Bedwyr had a brother."

"I only found out recently. Kid's been in a spot or two of bother, and still flits from job to job like a bumblebee. Bedwyr doesn't talk about him much. Though he loves the little shit." He shook his giant frame, for all the world like the dogs who were his most constant companions, and his smile resurfaced. "Anyway I'm off. Bedwyr has the evening free and the weather is so hot we're going skinny dipping in the river."

"Okay." Julia grinned at him. "But if you get arrested for indecent exposure don't expect me to stand bail."

He snorted out a laugh and left.

He must have met Angie in the hallway, because she appeared almost as soon as he had left.

Julia went to greet her young visitor, noticing how well a spring green tunic and skirt became her.

"Hello Angie. Thanks for coming."

Angie smiled. "It's on my way home, and I'd come a lot further for Cookie's food and Llewelyn Red." She looked at the pack of dogs that surrounded Julia. "I've never been this close to the black wolfhounds before. They weren't in the house much when I stayed here. They are handsome boys. What are they called?"

"Huginn and Muninn."

"For Odin's ravens?"

"Yes. And how clever of you to know."

Angie blushed, and Julia thought how little praise she probably got, which made Julia feel bad for how little she had even thought of Angie since the girl's wound had healed and she had gone back to her own home just after the turn of the year. Yes, her own life was busy, but in retrospect that didn't excuse what she now saw as a lack of care.

"Pour yourself a glass of wine and come out into the garden for a while."

Angie got a rather more modest glass than Julia's and they went out to where a stone bench stood in the sun. The dogs had noisy drinks before settling in the shade.

Angie laughed delightedly. "They look like a pile of legs and noses."

"Dai says an unmade bed."

There was a sudden pregnant pause.

"About Dominus Llewellyn…"

Julia laid a hand on Angie's arm. "Don't you be calling him Dominus. He'll be getting ideas above his station."

Angie hung her head miserably. "I was very silly about him when I first came here. Followed him from Londinium just because he was kind to me."

The sadness and bravery of that made Julia want to hug her, but she wasn't sure it would be a good idea.

"I can't argue with you about that. I'm silly about him too. And I followed him from Rome."

"Yes. But. You're his wife and he loves you."

"And you're his SI and he both likes and respects you a very great deal."

"Are you sure about that? See. He avoids me whenever he can."

Julia laughed. "He's a big coward. Knows you were a bit silly about him and doesn't know what to do about it. He values you highly so doesn't want to string you along, you see."

Angie looked at her with hope dawning in her eyes. "So he doesn't hate me?"

"No. Far from it. He thinks you are the best replacement for Bryn he could have had. He's had nothing but praise for the way you have been working."

"Maybe if he knew I'm not… well, not like that anymore…"

"Do you want me to tell him?"

"Oh, please, Domina Julia." Angie's voice was breathless with relief.

"It's just Julia. If we are going to be friends, and I think we are."

"Do you mean that?"

"I do. I also think I owe you an apology for not holding out the hand of friendship before."

For a second Angie looked as if she might have been going to cry, but she firmed her chin and essayed a wobbly smile.

"Does that mean I can come and see the dogs sometimes?"

"Course you can."

Angie beamed, and Julia felt even worse about how she and Dai had treated a lonely young woman. With a mental note to mark Dai's card firmly, Julia grinned at Angie.

"Sadly there's a bit of business that we need to get out of the way before we eat. I've been talking to the Praetor—or, more accurately, listening to him. We may have a problem. Or we may not."

Angie looked bewildered.

"Sorry. Basically the spados in Rome have lost sight of a couple of particularly dangerous praecipuum ponebaturs. For some undisclosed reason they think the carrion hunters are in Britannia. Maybe even here."

Angie nodded. "I hate those *twll dins*. They're evil and they don't care who gets hurt so long as they get paid."

"True. Which is why we're upping security a bit."

"Good. Do we know who?"

"Yes. I've got a printout for you."

Angie nodded and Julia got the feeling that a quick brain was sorting out implications and possible actions. She put her hand on Angie's arm.

"You'll do SI Ffrydd."

Angie's smile nearly split her face.

The sound of footsteps interrupted their 'girl talk'. Osian stood in the atrium looking entirely unsure of his welcome.

"Domina Julia, you did say…?"

Julia stood up. "I did. And it's Julia when we are off duty. Angie, this is my secretarius Osian."

"Pleased to meet you." Angie was polite but no more than that.

Julia led the way into the atrium, with Angie close behind her and she heard the girl's intake of breath when she stepped out of the sun and got her first good look at Osian.

Julia let Angie get beside her before she spoke again.

"Osian. This is SI Ffrydd."

"Angie please."

The two touched palms and Julia felt the electricity between them. She cursed inwardly, foreseeing an uncomfortable meal as chaperone between two people who suddenly appeared to have only one thing in mind. But she did them a disservice, as both were far too well brought up and professional to allow a jolt of sexual energy to divert them from their duties as guests. They ate and talked and laughed, although their eyes rarely left each other's faces, and if their sandalled feet weren't touching under the table Julia would be prepared to eat Edbert's woolly winter hat.

Being of a kindly nature, she shooed them away as soon as the food was eaten.

"Go on with you," she chuckled, "and Osian I think you should walk Angie home."

He blushed poppy pink, but he took Angie's hand in his. Julia went to the front door and watched for a small while as the two walked hand in hand. She rather thought the mile downhill to Angie's house wasn't going to cool their ardour too much. Then she went indoors and called Dai.

He answered at once, or, rather, their daughter answered.

"This is Aelwen, my Da's in the shower."

Julia repressed the desire to chuckle.

"What are you doing out of bed, missie?"

Aelwen's face appeared on screen. "Mam. I've been wanting and wanting you. Da promised to let me call so long as I was all ready for bed when he came out of the shower."

Julia could no more resist her daughter than she could fly.

"Well I suppose that's okay then. And I've been wanting you too."

Aelwen's smile went straight to her heart. "I'm all right now I've seen you. I can go to sleep."

Luned's face appeared beside Aelwen. "I didn't know you were missing your mam so much."

"No. Because I was being brave, like Da. But me and Rhodri, we have both been wanting her and wanting her."

Julia felt her heart swell. "Do you want to come home filia mia?"

Aelwen considered briefly before shaking her midnight curls. "No. I don't want Da to be missing me as well as you. I can manage if I can call you and say goodnight."

"I think we can arrange that." Julia said.

Luned nodded emphatically. "We can. Now blow your mam a goodnight kiss and give the wristphone to your da."

Aelwen blew kisses and Julia blew kisses too. Then the phone wobbled and Dai's face replaced Aelwen's.

He said nothing for a few seconds. "I didn't know Aelwen was missing you so badly."

"No. It's a bit of a surprise. Particularly given what a da's girl she is." He looked truly worried and Julia smiled. "It's all right, love. No harm done."

His face eased and he smiled into her eyes. "Aelwen was right about me missing you my love."

"Right back at you."

"Bloody job," he said moodily.

"You'd hate any other line of work."

He grinned. "I can't ever get anything past you can I? Which reminds me, can you check with Pina if we know officially that one Mamercinus Aemilius Lepidus is now resident on our patch? In Penllwyn."

"*Aemilius?*" Julia felt a slight tingle at the top of her spine. "The Aemilii are no friends to the Praetor."

Dai sighed. "I don't think there is anything much in it to worry about. He had Bryn over for a security consultation and I went along for the ride. Seems pretty harmless, just him and his daughter trying to put their lives

43

back together after he got free from being held prisoner of war for a decade. Looks like he's here because he couldn't handle the pressure of living in Rome. I did think Pina would want to know, though."

"I'll pass it on. But there is something else I need to tell you. Angie Ffrydd."

He swallowed. "You know I've been thinking about her. She really isn't a bad person, mean, I really quite like her and she's bloody good at her job. It's just…"

"Just you don't know how to handle the idea she may be after a bite of your most excellent ass."

"That's about the size of it."

Julia couldn't resist a giggle and Dai frowned. Before he could go off on one she dived straight on.

"Sorry. I couldn't help laughing. Thing is, I don't think you have to worry about Angie any more."

"You don't? Why?"

"Because I think you have been supplanted in her affections."

"How's that?" There was an odd note in Dai's tone.

Julia sniggered. "Jealous big boy?"

His laugh was strong and genuine. "No. Curious. Tell me."

"This evening I invited her round for cinio. To discuss bad people who may be on the horizon, and because I reckon we haven't been being fair to her."

"You might be right. And now I feel even more guilty. She's my SI but it took your intuition…"

Julia felt unable to take the credit. "Not my intuition. It was Gallus. He pointed out how we have been."

Dai's grin grew twisted. "Why do I keep underestimating that man?"

Julia lifted a shoulder, but she smiled. "Because when we first knew him he had buried himself so deeply there was only the rough tough mask of a Praetorian left. It's taken Olwen's love to soften his crusty shell and let the real man emerge."

"I just never seem to be able to let go of the original image…"

"Never mind, love. It will happen one day. So, you want to hear the good bit?"

"What good bit?"

"This evening I introduced Angie to Osian. And they went off hand in hand in search of a bed. If they made it past the haystack down the lane."

"Julia Llewellyn, what are you suggesting?" Dai sounded as though he didn't know whether to be shocked or amused.

"What I'm suggesting, Dai bach, is instalust. All through the meal he was looking at her as if he wanted to lick her face. Only good manners on both their parts kept them fully clothed and not rutting on my best carpet."

Dai burst out laughing. "Oh my goodness. And I missed that. But isn't she baby snatching?"

"No. He only looks young. He's actually thirty-one."

Dai was quiet for a dozen breaths. Then he spoke softly. "Well my darling wife, now you've got me all stirred up thinking about instalust I'm missing you even worse."

Julia smiled demurely. "Good. And Dai, we will be kinder to Angie won't we?"

Dai blew her a kiss. "We will. I just hope your secretarius can walk come morning."

After some small lovers' talk Julia ended the call and went to play ball with the dogs before it got too dark. Smiling.

III

For all the previous mornings of their time in Abermaw, Dai had been woken in his room in the delightful stone cottage he had rented for the duration, by two excited children. They would crawl onto and into bed demanding his attention and invention, until Luned came to get them dressed and ready for breakfast.

This morning he woke to the all too familiar sound of his wristphone and, bleary eyed, reached for it. Then suddenly he was wide awake and worried when he recognised the tone was the one that he'd set for Bryn. There was no good or happy reason he could imagine that Bryn would be calling him so early, but Bryn's face on the screen gave nothing away.

"Is everything al—"

"I'm fine, Bard, so is Gwen. But I can't say the same for Mamercinus Aemilius Lepidus."

Dai pushed himself up in bed.

"Something's happened to him?"

"I got a call just now from his daughter, Aemilia. She says he went out last night and didn't come back. She called the vigiles and was told that they could do nothing as he was a fully competent adult and had not been missing an unreasonable amount of time and besides, he had a bodyguard with him."

"She thinks otherwise?"

"She says her father has never vanished off like this before and is paying me good money to try and find him since the vigiles can't or won't."

Dai had to suppress the sudden thrill in his veins and realised he was like an old warhorse hearing the *cornu* trumpet. Then he remembered and he groaned.

"Bryn, I'm sorry, I just can't. Not today. Your day might be trying to trace a missing man, mine is ponies and donkeys and tractor trains and feeding animals. I promised to take the children to a local farm which caters for tourists to visit."

"No worries," Bryn sounded blasé about it, but Dai could tell there was a twist of disappointment the equal of the one he was feeling himself.

"Call me if something turns up."

"Will do. You have fun on the farm." Bryn smiled as if at a fond memory. "Not often your children get to monopolise you and I can promise you you'll regret missing out on that if you don't grab all the chances that come your way." Bryn, whose own brood had all now grown up and fled the nest, sounded sincere.

Finishing the call Dai decided it was too close to usual waking time to bother with trying to get back to sleep. So he got up and dressed, then forestalled the expected bed invasion by counter-invading the nursery just as the children were waking and created a happy uproar.

Just over an hour and a half-later, Dai was waiting outside the stone cottage when Bryn drew up in his all-wheel and opened the door.

"So what changed? I thought you were off to feed the goats and ride the donkeys?"

"I was," Dai agreed as he got in the vehicle and closed the door, "but then there was a breakfast argument which came to blows and Luned said that such naughty children couldn't possibly have such a treat today. It has been deferred on her cognisance, until the end of the week." He did not add that Luned had been just as scalding with him after the children had been packed off to their rooms. Apparently their poor behaviour was almost entirely down to him making them over-excited before breakfast. Fatherhood, Dai decided, was a lot tougher than it looked some days.

"Bread and water for lunch?" Bryn asked.

"I doubt it. Knowing Luned they will be out on the beach in less than an hour. I left her preparing a picnic for them."

"The man Duggan keeping an eye?"

Dai nodded. Having had his daughter dragged into his work and nearly dying as a result, he was glad to know that the invisible and efficient Duggan was there keeping his brood safe in his absence.

The journey back to Penllwyn was filled with a mixtur of speculation about why Aemilius might have gone missing and discussion of the news Gallus had given them about the bounty hunters at large in Britannia. On the latter topic, Bryn was in full agreement that the chances of such men having any reason to come to their small corner of the province was minute. Almost all world-class criminal activity was centred around Londinium after all.

This time, when they reached the villa they were waved through the outer gate and the barrier to the front of the house had been raised. Aemilia Aemilius Secunda herself was waiting at the portico and escorted them in personally.

Dai saw Bryn's gaze flick up briefly to the hated eagle above the lintel, before he stepped into the house.

Once they were alone in an elegant room with a sliding glass door that opened onto the atrium, her perfectly composed Roman patrician demeanour collapsed and she sank into a chair looking very young and vulnerable. Which, Dai supposed, was not so surprising. After all, she was now effectively alone in a province she did not know where the locals spoke a language she didn't understand and her father was missing.

As this was Bryn's shout Dai kept silent and let him run through the basic questions and answers.

No, her father didn't know anyone in the area as far as Aemilia was aware, or if he did he had not mentioned so to her. And no there were no places in particular she could recall him talking about. Yes, he had taken the hovercar, and yes, it was a very expensive one, a top of the range executive sports model.

No, she couldn't think of any enemies he might have, but then she didn't really know him very well or much about his life and work before he had been taken as a prisoner of war. After all she had been a very young child at that time.

Dai found his attention slipping from the quiet conversation as Bryn painlessly and efficiently extracted what little information she had from Aemilia. Looking around the room he noticed a letter discarded on a side table with a familiar logo emblazoned on it, resisting the impulse to stride over and pick it up, he waited until there was a pause in the questioning and cleared his throat.

"Domina Aemilius, I don't mean to pry, but I can't help but notice that you have a letter from the asclepieion on Ynys Mon. Is there some health issue that we might need to know about in relation to your father?"

It was a very long shot, but Dai had seen enough such envelopes sitting on his own desk with demands for payment following the intensive treatments that Julia and Rhodri had required following his son's birth.

A long shot, but one that found a mark.

Aemilia's mouth opened into a round O of surprise and epiphany, then her face flushed with colour.

"I hadn't thought of that. I know he had an appointment there sometime soon, but he didn't tell me he was going there yesterday and he always does. Besides, he would have come back straight after if that was where he went."

Bryn had picked up the envelope.

"May I?" he asked, holding it up.

Aemilia nodded.

"I have no idea why he is going there, he told me it was nothing to worry about and I believed him. But what if he has been taken ill? Or had an accident? Or if he—?" She was becoming increasingly upset as she no doubt followed her imagination through a sequence of ever more dire disaster scenarios.

Bryn was reading the letter and frowning at the page so Dai crossed swiftly to Aemilia and dropped into a crouch beside her, giving her his best vigiles smile. That was the one reserved for middle-aged matrons in distress. It usually had the effect of reassuring and distracting them.

Aemilia wasn't middle-aged but the smile still seemed to impact as she broke off what she had been about to say and blushed furiously.

"I'm sorry," she said and looked at her feet, "I'm just... just..."

"It's alright, domina," Dai told her soothingly. "It is only natural that you should be distressed and worried about your father."

"Who did have an appointment at the asclepieion late yesterday afternoon," Bryn told them, turning the page so they could both see. "It doesn't say for what or who with though. Only the time. But they can be very discreet in that place."

"I feel foolish now," Aemilia said. "I should have known that. But." She broke off and shook her head. "But that still doesn't explain why he has not come home."

"Perhaps," Dai suggested gently, "you could phone the asclepieion and ask if your father made it to his appointment and what time he left?"

As Aemilia made the call Dai found himself exchanging looks with Bryn. Aemilia was clearly not the sharpest knife in the cutlery draw.

The call was brief and unhelpful.

The asclepieion was unable to confirm or deny whether or not someone by the name of Aemilius had been seen there yesterday or any other day. Patient confidentiality was absolute and such records could only be accessed for such information with the permission of the client themselves. No one else, not even close family members.

When she finished the call, Aemilia had unshed tears of frustration and anger stark in her eyes.

"How can they not tell me? It is so unfair. My father could have been admitted unconscious and they wouldn't let me know."

"That is not very likely, domina," Dai assured her. "If he had been involved in any kind of accident they would have needed to inform the vigiles and then you would have been told."

Blowing her nose, Aemilia shook her head.

"So what do I do now?" she asked, sounding helpless.

Bryn was still holding the appointment letter and he tapped it with a finger.

"You don't need to do anything, Domina Aemilius. But if you will let me keep hold of this for the time being, we will go to Ynys Mons and ask in person if anyone saw your father there yesterday. Even if the asclepieion staff refuse to say anything, there may be those who saw his car. It is very distinctive."

He was rewarded with a sudden look of hope.

"Do you think so?"

"Oh yes, very," Bryn assured her.

"Did he take any staff member with him?" Dai asked. From what he had seen of the security conscious Aemilius he did not seem the kind of man to travel without a bodyguard in the wild depths of Britannia.

"Only Clovis, of course," she said as if it was obvious.

"Clovis?" Dai echoed.

"Oh. I forgot you won't have met him when you came before. He was out. But he is my father's driver and guard. Father would never go anywhere in the car without him."

So they were looking for two missing men and not just one.

A short time later, Dai was sitting beside Bryn as the all-wheel ate up the miles towards Ynys Mon.

"It really doesn't make a lot of sense," Bryn admitted. "I mean, I know the vigiles aren't going to raise the hue and cry for the man after such a short time, but you have to admit, Bard, it is a bit strange."

"I think I've learned enough about typical Roman Patrician behaviour to find nothing they do odd anymore," Dai told him. "I suspect we'll find he was attending some exclusive orgy and just forgot to turn his wristphone on. If he was at an allnighter he wouldn't be heading home until prandium. It wouldn't surprise me if he's either home or at least in touch with his daughter before we even get to Ynys Mon."

But when, a couple of hours later, they crossed the bridge to Ynys Mon, there had been no relieved call from Aemilia.

The only good news was that the young man overseeing the auto tolls did recall seeing the car Aemilius—or perhaps Clovis—had been driving. They called him over and he leaned on the lowered window to talk to them.

"*Cerbyd hyfryd*," he breathed, a look of longing in his eyes. "How could I possibly forget a beauty like that? We get a few real beauties through as there is the asclepieion and then that posh place, *Viridi Iugera Domus*, the private club for patricians, but they have a landing strip so it's not so many as choose to drive there, but no. I didn't notice who was in it. But that car, that car…"

"Did you see it return yesterday?"

"Not on my shift. I was here until midnight then on again six hours later. Covering for a friend, you see, he had to—"

"Do you have any video recordings?"

The young man looked suddenly uneasy.

"Well, yes, but we're not supposed to look at them."

"But you did," Dai said gently. It was so obvious it was painful. "You just wanted to see that car again."

"Well, I…"

Bryn reached into a pocket and waved some folding money towards the lad.

"It's none of anyone's business," he said, "but if you saw that car…"

"I didn't." The words held too much disappointment to be untrue and Bryn

Gave him a smile of consolation and some of the cash.

"You are doing a good job here," he said. "Have a tip."

As they took the road to the asclepieion, he shook his head and then looked across to Dai.

"Can't be that hard to find a car like that on a tiny island like this," he said, "surely."

***

Osian came to work with a beatific smile on his handsome face.

"Nice evening?" Julia enquired demurely.

His face flamed and she felt a pang of remorse.

"It's all right. I'm only teasing."

Osian smiled. "I need to man up about this. I know it's sudden and all that, but I think I knew the moment I set my eyes on Angie. And she feels the same way too."

"Angie has been very much alone and if she has found someone to care for her, then I'm pleased. Pleased on both your accounts. But Osian…"

He held up a hand. "You have no need to worry, Domina Julia. Angie and I are aware that this may not last but we have decided we want to find out. And I promise I will never hurt her by word or deed."

"Good. That's all I needed to know. Now. Work."

He grinned and went to his desk.

It proved to be a morning full of frustration, culminating in Julia pulling rank on the manager of a small, private bank in Viriconium when he refused to divulge details of Moley's finances. The threat of a detachment of praetorian guards coming to check out his premises changed his attitude and Osian's printer was soon chattering merrily.

He brought a sheaf of papers to Julia with a sober face.

"What?"

"I know a bit about this bank. According to my previous employer it's where you put money when you don't want the *tributum officium* to get wind of it."

Julia grinned. "It's no wonder the idea of praetorian interest made the man so unhappy then."

"Yes. But domina, there are very bad people involved. If they think you are sticking your nose in their business."

"It's okay. I'm well protected. And if the manager gets a slap from his employers I find myself unable to worry too much about the fate of a petty thief."

He looked at her open mouthed for a minute, then grinned. "Dominus Paulus said you were ruthless in the pursuit of ill doers, I see now how right he was."

"That's as maybe but…" Her wristphone shrilled importantly. "That's Angie. Emergency code. I need to answer. Julia here."

Angie's voice came through slightly breathlessly. "Sorry. I've been running. Lost the irrumators though. Anyway. I was on my way to the Dog and Onion having had a message that herself wanted a word, although turns out it was only to assure me she and hers had no hand in the present spate of thefts. Anyway, I was almost there when I saw a scuffle in a doorway. Almost ignored it, but then I realised it was two big guys kicking the merda out of a woman. So I intervened. Just as well I did. It's Caeso Maol's housekeeper. She's in a bit of a state. Says they were demanding to know where he put the goods. I'd say she really doesn't have any idea what they were on about."

"How is she?"

"No bones broken I can see. They'd not had time to get warmed up. She's in the back room of the Dog getting first aid whilst the owner is spitting blood about someone trying to muscle in on her turf. I'm on my way back there now."

"You're not on your own are you?"

Angie showed her teeth in a wicked grin. "What? Round here? No chance. She moved her wristphone to show two large vigiles conspicuously armed with clubs.

"Good. I'm on my way in. But I think a stop at Maol's house on the way."

Angie nodded. "Should I have the housekeeper brought to HQ?"

"Please. And have a proper medicus take a look at her."

"Will do."

Angie was gone and Julia felt her most feral grin crossing her face. "Osian. Will you buzz Gallus and Edbert? Tell them we're going out. And I want all four dogs."

He nodded and she shot out of the room.

Inside five minutes she was back, having parked Domina Julia Llewellyn in the wardrobe with her light summer tunica and pulled out Julia the street fighter in leather trews and waistcoat with hard boots on her small feet and a pistol at her hip.

Gallus was already there. He looked her over sharply and nodded. "Edbert and the dogs should be in the all-wheel awaiting us."

Julia got the distinct impression he'd know the reason why if they weren't. She turned her attention to Osian.

"This house is on lockdown until I return. Elfrida knows what to do. Will you please message Domina Cariad and say I may be late?"

He bowed his assent and Julia and Gallus moved out fast.

Of course Edbert and the dogs were in the vehicle and the gun rack in the back was full.

"Where to?" The man mountain asked, although Julia would have been willing to make a modest wager that the question was purely for form's sake.

"Caeso Maol's house. I'll just look it up."

"No need. I know the way."

Guessing what sort of a ride she was in for, Julia tightened her seatbelt and grabbed the leather handle that hung at her side. She was only just in time because once the vehicle was out of the gates of the villa, Edbert floored it. Even Gallus held on tight when they left the metalled road and barrelled up a barely discernible path across the heathland. The dogs understood that this was going to be a wild ride and sensibly positioned themselves in the rear footwell around Gallus' big, booted feet. He laughed, and Lupo rested a paw on his thigh.

Once her internal organs had rearranged themselves in such a way as to be able to cope with the bouncing and jostling of this mode of travel, Julia turned a mildly inquiring gaze on Edbert.

"What lit a fire up your backside?"

He spared her a grin. "Gallus said we were in a hurry. Besides which, life has been a bit too sedate of late."

Julia huffed out a laugh. "For how long do I have to endure my spleen having a fist fight with my tonsils?"

"About ten minutes then we cut back into the highway. We should be at our destination in twenty or so."

Once they got back onto the metalled road the ride improved sufficiently that Julia no longer needed to be careful not to bite her tongue. She screwed round in her seat to look at Gallus who had Huginn on his lap.

"I don't know." He answered her unspoken question.

"He must have felt sick down on the floor. On your lap he has air flow but he still feels safe." Edbert chuckled. "He probably won't throw up."

"If he does, I can point his head towards the back of your neck."

Julia shook her head. "How close can we get before we are seen, Gallus?"

He consulted his wrist unit's bank of drone footage. "If we come in from the north pretty well up to the house. Unlike the *Villa Papaverus*, it's not walled all round. It looks to be a pseudo-Roman building, but the portico is in the east face of the block and the woods come right down to within metres of the north wall. Not very defensible."

"It was probably built like that for some reason other than defensibility."

"Yeah. It's to do with the view. Bedwyr and I walked over the hill and saw the place one day. He told me why it's built that way, and that it's one of the many places Beynon's managed to lose a job in during his short life."

"Beynon?"

"Bedwyr's kid brother."

"Oh, yes. The one you don't think deserves to be loved."

"Yes. Him." Edbert grunted his disgust.

As they grew closer to their destination, Julia got the strongest possible prod from her detective intuition.

"I think we're too late boys."

Edbert didn't slow down, though he did spare her a glance. "Got a feeling in your bones have you?"

"Yup. I'm thinking this may not be very nice."

As it turned out, not very nice was a bit of an understatement. The all-wheel screeched to a halt shooting up plumes of gravel and dust and the first sign of trouble was the front door hanging drunkenly on one hinge. Or, rather more accurately, bits of shattered wood hanging where there would once have been a door.

"Call it in Gallus."

He tapped his wristphone. "SI Gallus requesting backup. Code red. Villa Talpa. Forced entry." He listened for a minute before snarling. "If you would like to have a word with Domina Julia, she's right here. No? I thought not. Damage report? From where I'm sitting now the front doors have been blown in. Mortar at a guess."

"Who?"

"One of the civilians who was trying to claim a shedload of overtime she hadn't done."

"Oh. I see. Do mark her card firmly when you have a spare moment. Nobody argues with any officer in need of backup. Now. What do we think? Do we go in? Or wait?"

"In, I think. The bad guys are gone."

Edbert got out of the vehicle and bulked his shoulders. "I'll watch your back."

"Keep Canis and Lupo with you. I'll take the babies in with me."

Julia, Gallus, Huginn and Muninn moved into a scene of utter devastation, there seemed to be nothing in the entrance or the atrium that hadn't been deliberately smashed. Even the household gods in their niche were headless and crumbling. Gallus swore briefly under his breath and Julia followed the direction of his eyes. Somebody's pet cat lay disembowelled on the floor. Julia looked away and the quartet kept moving on silent feet. Where a tapestry had been dragged from the wall, the dogs stopped pointing to the pile of cloth. Julia lifted a corner to be confronted by a pair of terrified eyes. The child couldn't have been more than three or four and he crouched motionless. Julia put out a hand and he flinched away, she didn't attempt to move any closer. Instead she spoke in a calm and quiet voice.

"It's all right now. The bad people have gone."

"All gone?"

"Yes."

He pointed to Huginn and Muninn. "Dogs?"

"Yes, little man."

She motioned the boys closer and they came on soft feet. The child wrapped his arms around Huginn's neck and began to sob heart wrenchingly. Julia let him cry for a while before placing a gentle hand on his head. He turned into her arms and she lifted him. Gallus was instantly at her side, with a big soft handkerchief at the ready. He mopped the little boy's face.

"What's your name *dyn bach*?"

Julia put away the strangeness of Gallus speaking the local argot to be considered later, instead concentrating on the job in hand.

"Dilwyn."

"Well, Dilwyn. Let's get you outside where you can sit in the sunshine with a very big man and two more dogs to stop you from being afraid, shall we?"

Dilwyn put a hand in Gallus' big, scarred palm and the three of them went out to where Edbert waited by the all-wheel.

"This is Dilwyn," Gallus said, "he's been a very brave man, but now he needs somebody to keep the *gwillions* away."

Edbert smiled. "They won't get past me and the boys. Dilwyn, these are Canis and Lupo and I'm Edbert."

Dilwyn smiled and Julia passed him into Edbert's care.

The quartet went back into chaos, and Julia was beginning to wonder whether Dilwyn was the only soul left living when her ears caught the muffled sound of sobbing.

"Find."

Huginn and Muninn looked at her intelligently and turned tail, within seconds they were scratching at a door that was partially concealed by an overturned bookcase. She and Gallus dragged the heavy thing a couple of feet and he kicked the door lock once, twice, and on the third kick it burst open revealing the head of a stone staircase.

"It's all right," Julia called, "we're here to help. The bad guys have gone and we're the first of the *achubwyr*."

"You've come to help us?"

The voice was female and educated Romano-British, but edged with pain.

"Yes. We're on our way down." Julia looked at Gallus. "First aid kit please."

He went at speed and Julia cautiously descended the stairs. At the bottom there was a light, bright room with slot windows high in the walls. Inside the room there were a dozen or so women. Most bore bruises and abrasions as witness to having been treated roughly at the very least. Three were in a much worse case. The oldest, who sat with her back against the wall with an obviously broken arm in her lap, was a little better dressed than the rest and Julia guessed she was the lady of the house.

"Domina Maol?" she hazarded.

"I am, but if you think I have any idea what all this was about…"

"I don't. I'm Submagistratus Julia Llewellyn."

The woman relaxed. "Then we really are safe."

Julia was suddenly hit with a thunderbolt of thought. Gallus came down the stairs at a dead run and she showed him her teeth. "We need to call Angie."

"Why."

"Maol's warehouses."

"Merda. I'm on it."

He clattered back up the stairs.

"Now then. I have antiseptic and soothing ointment for minor cuts and bruises, but we could truly do with some water."

A youngish girl with an impressive black eye stood up. She ran her tongue around her teeth.

"There's a pump down here."

She pointed to a corner and Julia turned that way.

"I can get it, domina, and deal with the minor injuries if you would look to our *arglwyddes* and the other two who were worse hurt."

There was little Julia could do for the broken arm, save give Domina Maol a painkiller and carefully slide a soft fleece blanket under the injured arm. A very pretty woman who was whimpering quietly seemed to Julia to have a broken jaw. One of the others looked at her in some pity.

"She has a little boy and she's afraid they've taken him."

"Would that be Dilwyn?"

The injured woman managed to nod.

"He's fine. Outside in an all-wheel, with my bodyguard and a couple of wolfhounds for company."

The young mother sagged and Julia found an ampoule of opiate. "I'm going to give you something for the pain," she said firmly.

With Dilwyn's mam sorted there was just a girl with a bitter self-pitying twist to her lips who glared at Julia from hate-filled eyes.

"Now then *puella*, let's have a look at you."

The girl tried to draw in a breath and her face paled.

"Ribs," Julia muttered.

She carefully opened the girl's tunic to see her torso covered in contusions, many of which were weeping sullenly.

"Kicked you, did they?"

The girl gave up her bitter world-weary pose. "Yes." Even that word cost her a huge effort and Julia got out another needle.

"I can give you a shot to help with the pain."

"Please."

With the three worst injured settled, Julia looked around.

"Can anyone tell me what happened here?"

The girl with the black eye lifted a shoulder. "It's all a bit confused. Brangwen went off to do the marketing as usual. Goes off at dawn, she does. The rest of us were just waking up when there's a bang and the front doors come in in pieces. Then the house was full of men. Asking questions and beating us for not knowing the answers."

"What sort of questions?"

"Only one really, variations on a theme. Where did the Dominus keep the goods?"

"Only we didn't know what goods." Another voice broke in. "After a while they left most of us and concentrated on those three. Dominus Caeso's wife, his niece, Elin, and his leman, Sionedd."

"And how did they know who was who?"

"That's a very good question. And I don't know the answer. None of us told them. Did we?"

There was a chorus of no's.

Julia believed them. Somebody somewhere had betrayed these women, and she was beyond angry.

Sionedd was making an effort to speak, through the pain in her stoved in ribs. Julia put a hand on her chest.

"Breathe shallowly, *merch*."

"They said a name," Sionedd whispered. "Beynon."

Julia's mind went back to the conversation in the all-wheel, even as the girl with the black eye hissed.

"That wouldn't surprise me at all." She turned her face to Julia. "As you can see there aren't a lot of men in this household. But the master brought home a handsome young lad one day last winter. Said the lad was wasted in his warehouses and he was going to train him up as a secretarius. Snooper more like. Stayed about a month, then just disappeared."

"Casing the joint." The speaker was a broad-hipped middle-aged woman who Julia thought must be the household cook. "I knew he was a bad lot the minute I set my eyes on him. And I should know about bad lots. My whole family's bad news." Then she shut her mouth like a rat trap.

Julia saw no need to challenge her, particularly when she saw the state of the woman's right hand.

"What'd they burn you with?"

"Lamp oil, domina."

Julia furgled about in her first aid kit for a cooling pack. When she found it she snapped the ampoules inside and as soon as the soft gel cooled sufficiently she held it out.

"Put your hand in here. It'll help."

"Oh my goodness. What's in that thing?"

"I honestly don't know, but do I know it cools burns even better than ice water."

"It does."

"You just sit still and let it do its work. You look a bit shock-y to me."

"More than a bit." Gallus spoke from behind Julia's shoulder. "Medical help should be here any minute. Vigiles are on the road and they won't be long either."

As if to prove him a true prophet the sound of helicopter rotors split the air.

Julia's wristphone squawked.

"Helimed zero nine coming in to land."

Gallus sprinted up the stairs and the girl with the black eye looked impressed.

"He's fit for an old guy."

Julia grinned. "Ex-praetorian."

The girl whistled through her teeth. "Here?"

"Yes. He came for a special job, fell in love, and stayed."

"Fell in love?" Most of the women eyed Julia speculatively.

She laughed. "He fell in love with my husband's mam."

Three 'flying nurses' clattered down the stairs.

"What do we have here?"

Julia pointed out the three with broken bones and the cook with the burnt hand, who was getting paler by the minute. The medics took over and Julia was able to start helping the rest up the staircase and through the ruined house to the sunshine and the chairs someone had found for them.

The sound of a labouring engine announced the arrival of an all-wheel with a half dozen vigiles aboard. The men all saluted Julia.

"Domina Julia."

"Right lads, it's just really a mop-up job. Make sure we haven't missed anything or anybody."

They all nodded. Their de facto leader spoke.

"The door's toast. What's it like inside?"

"Unpleasant."

The youngest vigiles swallowed audibly, being well aware that Julia wasn't given to exaggeration. One of the older men patted his shoulder.

"You'll be fine. Just keep with me."

The vigiles went inside, stopping to speak to Gallus as he came out, more or less carrying the lady of the house. He brought her over to Julia, who felt a stab of pity.

"I'm sorry for your trouble, domina. Be assured we will do our best to find out who is responsible."

"Thank you for your concern, and for the help you have already given us." She looked at the ruined front door of her home and sighed. "It's as well I never really liked the house." Squaring her thin shoulders she spoke up bravely. "My husband was in the habit of cheating his business associates, and I can only assume that whoever those gentlemen were they were employed by was one of those. It makes me very grateful that I have always retained control of my own money."

She held out her uninjured hand and she and Julia touched knuckles.

Once everything possible had been done and Dilwyn had kissed all the dogs goodbye before going off in the ambulance with his mother's friends, Julia climbed into her own vehicle and sighed. For the first time she had leisure to look at Edbert. There was a muscle jumping in one lean cheek and his mouth was set in a thin, hard line.

"Penny for them mammoth."

"The little man mentioned a name."

"Ah yes. Beynon. One of the worst treated girls said his name came up in what I guess we'll just have to call conversation. I'd rather like a word with him if he can be located."

Edbert's big hands flexed on the steering wheel. "I'll put my mind to it."

Behind them Gallus grunted. "If you need any help."

Edbert relaxed enough to turn his head and grin wolfishly.

"Do remember I'd like him in a condition to talk," Julia said softly.

Both men laughed, although it wasn't a sound that boded any good to Beynon if either or both got their hands on him.

Julia's wristphone burbled. It was Angie. Her face was dirty, looking to be besmirched with soot.

"Warehouses have gone up in smoke. Though at least we got there in time to prevent any fatalities. Same story as Gallus said you're dealing with. Big angry people wanting to know where the 'consignment' is."

Julia sighed. "It would help if we even knew what the gods-cursed consignment was."

"It would. I'm now going back to the Dog and Onion. I reckon herself was protesting too much, if she knows something I'm in no mood to dance around her."

"Be careful Angie. That place is dangerous."

Angie showed her teeth. "I'm going in mob-handed. And unlike Dai I feel no particular compulsion to be gentlemanly."

They shared a vicious grin and Angie ended the call.

"She'll do just fine," Gallus all but purred.

Julia sort of thought she should say something about justice and citizens rights, but found when it came to the likes of Aiofe and Brangwen Broanan, the leaders of one of the most brutal criminal enterprises in Viriconium, she couldn't be bothered. Instead she sat back and listened to a thought that had been itching at the back of her head.

"I think we're missing something," but she spoke ruminatively and the men stayed quiet. Thinking back over the events of the past couple of hours she tried to look more carefully at everything and everybody. At first it felt like groping in the dark, but then she saw a badly burned hand in her mind's eye. Why had the cook been singled out for such torture? She was hardly in a position to be in her master's confidence. So why? The answer when it came to her was very simple.

"I know what I was missing now. It's the cook. The woman with the burnt hand. The burn was by way of a warning to keep her mouth shut."

"You've lost me there filia mia."

"She mentioned coming from less than virtuous roots. I reckon she knew at least one of the attackers."

Edbert nodded. "We going to ask her?"

"No. There is no point. No matter what we threatened she'd not tell. She knows what her life and that of her loved ones would be worth if she did. However, we can at least be sure that whoever Maol cheated is using local labour."

"We can. Let's see what Angie digs up."

"In the meantime, let's go home."

IV

It was reaching past time for prandium when Dai and Bryn pulled up in the asclepieion visitors car park.

Ten minutes later, as Bryn was being stonewalled by the smiling receptionist, whose name tag declared was called Domhnall, Dai began to wonder if he should try introducing himself as the submagistratus. But even as he opened his mouth to do so he realised it was not a good idea at all. Either Domhnall would then fall over himself to provide the information, placing Dai in the difficult position of having to justify his action on invoking his rank whilst on effective, if not actual, suspension. Or, worse, the receptionist might call his bluff and demand it be made official and then Dai would have to admit it was not.

So he said nothing as Bryn was politely informed that even if the gentleman he was enquiring about was indeed a client of the asclepieion—which Domhnall was neither in a position to conform not yet deny—it would be contravening their confidentiality best practice guidelines to say anything about him whatsoever to anyone.

Bryn was clearly grinding his teeth as they walked through the doors that swished open as they approached then sighed shut behind them.

"He was here," Bryn growled, as they got back into the vehicle, "I could just tell by the self-satisfied, withholding, cunnus smirk or that spado's face."

Dai had to agree.

"Then at least our journey was not completely wasted," he pointed out.

Bryn gave him a filthy look and made a harumphing sound. Dai laughed and then stopped as he heard a small hiss and an odd sweetness filled his nose.

Beside him Bryn had been about to start the vehicle but now shook his head and looked as if he might be about to say something when Dai found himself slipping backwards, as if through his seat and then back and back into a long dark tunnel.

He woke up feeling as if a man with a hammer was stuck between his eyes and struggled to move, before realising his ankles and wrists had been secured with cable ties.

"You might not want to do that." The voice was cultured and precise, the classic voice of a Roman bureaucrat.

Blinking Dai realised he was in some kind of stone shed, probably a disused byre or bothy. The walls were undressed stone and the roof rough slates pinned on old rafters. There was a single window which let in enough light to see the room was empty aside from an old mattress, some empty cans and bottles, himself, Bryn who was also cable tied and starting to stir, and an elegantly dressed Roman who stood watching them both, a pistol held almost casually in one hand.

"Those ties are designed to tighten if you pull too hard," the man said helpfully. "And I do apologise for the inconvenience, Submagistratus Llewellyn, and Ex-Senior Investigator Cartivel."

Dai stopped pulling on his bonds and wriggled himself into a sitting position , grateful for the wall behind him. He realised that they must have been unconscious for several hours as there was now very little sunlight coming in through the filthy window.

"You clearly know who we are," he said coldly, determined not to let their captor hold any more of the initiative than he had to, "so who are you?"

"My name is Vinculus," the man said, "Reponerus Vinculus Septimus. Only you won't find my name listed in any official sources. I am one of the *Novem*, the nine elite secret agents employed personally by the emperor to deal with matters that touch the honour of the Divine family."

Eying the pistol which Vinculus now held across his chest, Dai wondered if he was dealing with a fanatic or a fantasist.

"Never heard of them," Bryn said, stealing the words Dai had been about to speak.

Vinculus gave a slight smile.

"Well, no. Of course you haven't. We would hardly be very secret if you had, would we?"

"Septimus. Let me guess," Dai said, knowing how all Roman officialdom lacked any imagination, "the others are Primus through Nonum? You are the seventh of nine?"

"Indeed so, submagistratus. And before we have a little chat about what exactly you two were doing asking after Mamercinus Aemilius Lepidus at the asclepieion, I should also inform you that we are also all designated to be an *Operativus Occisor*."

Beside Dai, Bryn drew a sharp breath.

"Killer operatives?"

Dai had heard rumours of such men, trusted enough to make life and death decisions on their own initiative when protecting the empire. It meant he could kill both Dai himself and Bryn and face no comeback for doing so—except maybe a dressing down if it was found he had made the wrong call.

For the first time since he had woken Dai felt a thin thread of terror work its way through his veins.

"Yes. I am designated Operativus Occisor Septimus. I have the emperor's own licence to kill if I deem it necessary. And that licence covers any other action I might need to take in the course of my mission as well."

"The Praetor—" Dai's voice cracked as he spoke and his throat was too dry.

"The Praetor has no say over what I do, I am sorry to tell you. And he would have no knowledge of this as it is the Emperor's own business affecting his own family. My job is to make sure any such problems are simply removed so no taint of scandal can ever touch the Emperor himself. So, although I know you are under praetor's patronage, that will not help you here." His lips tightened into a predatory smile. "No. The only thing that can help you now is complete honesty—that is assuming that you are not actually in league with the Mongolian Empire."

"Of course we're not!" Dai found himself propelled from fear into anger at the thought. "Why would you consider for a moment that we were?"

Bryn gave a groan.

"Let me guess," he said, "Mamercinus Aemilius Lepidus is a spy for the Mongol Empire?"

"Are you sure that is a guess, Cartivel?" There was an edge in Vinculus tone and the pistol moved to point to Bryn's chest.

"Course it's a guess. How was I to know the *irrumator* was a spy? I never even heard of him before he hired me to look over the locks and bolts on his doors."

"So why did he pick you rather than any other local security consultant? And why," he made a sharp gesture towards Dai, "did you happen to take along the local submagistratus for such a job?"

Dai's mind reeled. He could see now how suspicious that would seem to someone who didn't know the whole situation... And then to turn up here…

"He hired Bryn, we were told, because he wanted a local man who understood the local people. I went along because I," had nothing better to do and was getting a bit bored on vacation? He changed his mind without even a momentary hesitation, "am truly a local and Bryn might be British but he is a Londinium man through and through. However as it turned out that made no difference, Aemilus merely wanted a security checkup."

Vinculus nodded then laughed briefly. "Yes. Of course. A man who is one of the top experts on security in the Mongolian Empire, with his own people around him, asks a local PI to come and make sure his CCTV is placed correctly."

"It wasn't him," Bryn said. "It was his daughter who insisted."

Vinculus moved the hand not holding the gun and Dia saw an oddly dull gold ring of citizenship on the index finger, dull but a little larger than the usual with a smooth face that suddenly turned black and a small image appeared on it as if it were a screen. Even at the distance he was, Dai could see the sleek outline of the car they had followed to Ynys Mon. A moment later it had vanished and there was an image of Aemilia Aemilius there instead.

"That's the daughter," he said and a moment later the image was gone and the ring looked plain again. "She also hired us to find her father after he didn't come home last night and hadn't been in touch. She was very worried about him. The only clue we had was that he had an appointment letter for the asclepieion. I'm sure you will have found it if you searched us. And that's a nice ring."

"It is," Vinculus agreed, seeming perhaps a little less hostile than before. "There were only nine ever made and they are very special. Unique, even.The emperor himself has the master ring that controls all these. It gives him direct communication with us. Just not the other way around."

He moved his hand again and the ring became a regular dull gold again. It took Dai a moment more to realise that Vinculus had also put the pistol back in the shoulder holster he wore under a jacket.

"You've decided not to kill us then?" he hazarded.

"No." Vinculus sounded almost disappointed, Dai thought. "Having let the Q-puter analyse the available data I'm getting a reading that suggests a high nineties probability that you are telling the truth. Something I concur with as you seem pretty harmless and fell for one of the oldest tricks in the book, not even checking your vehicle when you got in it." He shook his head as if saddened by such evident amateurism. "And besides, I need some help and you two seem to be the best option I have available at the moment, may the Divine Diocletian help me. So no, I'm not going to kill you, I'm going to recruit you."

***

Julia had time for a quick shower and a brief conversation with Aelwen before her sister-in-law Cariad arrived.

As always, when they had been apart for a while, Cariad's beauty as she came into the atrium just about took Julia's breath away.

"How in the name of all the gods do you do it?"

"Do what?" Cariad laughed.

"Always manage to be lovely to behold."

"Oh. That. Just a lot of hard work and a very wealthy husband who never grudges any of the enormous amounts of money I expend on my vanity."

She held out her arms and they hugged tremendously.

"Anyway Julia fach, you are certainly a lady who improves with age yourself. You are a tiny bit rounder since Aelwen and Rhodri and it suits you mightily. Also you look good enough to eat in pink, which I envy you as it makes me look like a drag artiste."

Julia grinned. "It's the hair, my friend. Not even the most stunning redhead on two continents can carry pink."

Cariad grinned like the apple-scrumping urchin she still was at heart. "Oh. I've missed you."

"Right back at you."

They gravitated to the table where cookie had outdone herself, and there was a bottle of the sparkling red wine Dai and Cariad's brother, Hywel, had just perfected. Over dinner they chattered and giggled as if they had seen each other only yesterday rather than the year that had passed. They swapped stories of their husbands and children, and Julia told Cariad all about Angie and how Dai had been superseded in that young woman's affections.

It was late, and Edbert came out to the garden where the two women sat watching fireflies.

"Your chariot awaits, Domina Cariad."

Cariad laughed. "And if I don't hustle along, you'll just carry me."

He grinned but didn't contradict her merely turning on his heels and heading for the front door, the two women followed him giggling like schoolgirls. They hugged for a few minutes before Cariad got into the all-wheel.

"See you soon, sister mine. Enya and Hywell want you, Dai and the children to come over just as soon as you can."

Edbert put the vehicle in gear and it slid noiselessly away.

Julia stood on the gravel at the bottom of the steps up to the portico, watching until the vehicle's tail lights were out of sight. She couldn't help thinking that it was a minor miracle how a good kick up the backside from life had morphed the spoilt wife of a wealthy Roman into the warm, lovely woman Cariad was now. Which led her to wonder how she herself, a child of the suburra, who was street fighter to the bone, had come to fall for a poet with added angst. And, moreover, how in the name of all the gods did such a relationship even begin to work. She knew that kind of introspection did nobody any good and mentally shrugged her shoulders, although she did wonder how she was going to get through a husband and children-less night without shedding a few tears.

"Bugger it," she muttered to herself as she set her foot on the bottom step. When she was half turned, a pair of merciless hands grasped her arms and she was dragged back against a hard chest.

"Domina Llewellyn. Keep your eyes forward. Don't try to look at me and you won't get hurt too much."

Julia kept still—except for the hand that slid into her pocket and gripped the tiny antique pistol that Dai had bought her for their last anniversary.

"Oh, good. A sensible woman. I have a message for you."

"You do?" Julia kept her voice light and even.

"Be quiet and listen."

He moved fast bringing his right hand hard around her throat while his left wrist moved in front of her eyes. The screen of one of the two wristphones he wore came to life, and a dark harsh-featured face looked at her coldly.

"I have some instructions for you Domina Llewellyn," the voice was coldly unpleasant and entirely without the musicality that marked out the locals. Julia carefully marked each feature of his face, burning them into her memory. He stared at her as if he was doing the same thing.

"You are to keep silent and listen."

Julia rather thought she had been keeping silent and began to understand that her calmness was somehow unexpected and unwelcome. She allowed nothing to show in her face, though.

"You and your petty little vigiles are getting in my way, and I am not a man who puts up with inconvenience. You will step back from the investigation of Caeso Moal's demise. It is none of your business." He was now breathing heavily and Julia felt the heat of his anger even through the tiny face of a wristphone. "I am sure you have no intention of obeying me, but before you do anything stupid you might want to consider the fate of a group of mongol slavers who were exterminated for taking you as a slave. Their leader had a younger brother, who has now grown up and is offering a great deal of gold for the whereabouts of the female he holds responsible for his brother's death. I just have to make one call and a nice little bit of torture and murder is on order if you don't do as you are told."

It was Julia's turn to feel anger, but hers was cold and she knew nothing showed in her face.

"Do you have nothing to say for yourself, woman?"

The hand about Julia's throat tightened enough that she would have had difficulty speaking even if she wanted to.

"Very well. Beynon. Hurt the lady—just to make sure she knows I mean what I say."

His face turned intent as if he was about to enjoy some entertainment, but it never materialised .

Julia was now beyond angry and she wasn't about to let anyone get away with outright threats. Her captor might have thought himself quick, but compared to an angry Julia he was as slow as Aelwen's pet tortoise. Before he could move a whisker, she pulled the little gun from her pocket and shot him in the leg. He screamed, high and thin and dropped her as if she was a poisonous snake. She grabbed his wrist and glared into the screen of the wristphone.

The harsh-faced man snarled. "You have just signed your own death warrant."

"I think not. What I have done is served notice on you. I just kneecapped your boy. And when I find you, which I will, I promise to do the same to you. Both knees, I think. Run away now, and hide. And spend the rest of your life looking over your shoulder. Because I will be there."

He managed to meet her obsidian gaze for about three heartbeats before the realisation that this was no idle threat hit him. His face disappeared.

Julia noticed that the screaming behind her had stopped, and turned to see her housekeeper's sons Bran and Col kneeling beside the injured man.Canis and Lupo were standing half a foot away with their teeth bared.

"The dogs said there was something—and we came," Bran explained.

"Will he survive?" Julia asked, and her voice sounded harsh and scratchy in her ears.

"For a while." Col said. "He isn't even bleeding much. But I don't give a lot for his chances once Edbert gets his hands on him."

"Talking of Edbert and household security of which he is in charge. Do we have any idea how this piece of ordure got in here?" Julia was now fighting for composure and didn't dare look at the now quietly sobbing man, for fear of doing something regrettable.

"We do. He looks like Bedwyr, and he's wearing Bedwyr's wrist unit."

"He's Bedwyr's brother so the resemblance is easily explained. But what about the wrist unit?" Julia raised a brow and Bran took over.

"All of us servants come and go via the back gate. There's facial recognition and everyone has an identity chip in their wristphone."

"Oh I see. I do hope Bedwyr didn't give his wristphone to Beynon here."

The sound of an all-wheel being driven entirely too fast split the night.

"I think we're about to find out."

The headlights of the all-wheel raked the front of the house and it had barely stopped when Edbert and Gallus leapt out.

Edbert rubbed a hand over his face.

"Are you hurt, small stuff?"

"A bit bruised but I'll live."

Gallus didn't waste time on words. He was at Julia's side in a dozen huge strides and he pulled her into a rough embrace. For about twenty seconds she allowed herself to burrow into his strong arms, then she stiffened her spine and turned to lean her back against his chest.

"Edbert," she said, proud of how little tremor there was in her voice, "talk."

"I was just dropping Domina Cariad at the farm, when my wristphone squawked. I didn't recognise the ID, so I nearly let it go unanswered but then I got the willies. So I picked up. It was Bedwyr. In a state. At first I couldn't get much sense. Then I understood this *futator* here had nicked his wristphone, so I scooped up Gallus and broke the land speed record." Then he came to where Julia stood in the circle of Gallus' arms. He knelt down so his eyes were level with hers. "I let you down, Julia. I'm sorry."

The pain in his deep-set eyes made her stomach hurt and she put a hand on his shoulder.

"Don't be stupid, Edbert. It wasn't your fault. It wasn't even Bedwyr's fault. But this little irrumator... Words fail me."

Gallus squeezed her gently, signalling his approval. "She's right Edbert. Less self flagellation, more action."

Edbert's huge body relaxed. He looked at Julia and smiled. She offered him a grin. As she turned her head to look up at Gallus, the light must have caught her throat and Edbert swore.

"You said a bit bruised. Your throat is a mess."

Gallus turned her so he could look for himself.

"That has to be sore."

"I expect it will be when I come down. But right now I'm running on adrenaline and fury. Beynon's boss rather thought he could lay down the law to me, specifically, prohibiting me from investigating Caeso Maol's murder. And to make it stick he threatened to sell my whereabouts to the brother of Chingis of the Manghud."

"Did he indeed?"

"He did and this cunnus here was about to hurt me to show they are in earnest."

Bran waved a very large fist under Beynon's nose. "I really don't like you," he said and Beynon's whimpering grew louder.

"I'm bleeding," he sobbed. "I could die."

Edbert took two big strides to his head. "If you are very lucky we might let you do just that."

Julia became aware that there were a great many things she should be doing about Beynon, like formally arresting him, and getting him proper medical attention, and questioning him closely—but she was suddenly tired.

Gallus could have read her mind as he bent his head to her ear.

"It would be easiest if you never saw him."

His voice was softly teasing, although Julia heard the 'but' that underpinned what he said. Which was, if you happened to have sufficient time to think about it, quite a volte face from a former praetorian guard who had never needed to so much as consider the rights of ordinary folks—until he joined the vigiles.

She managed a tired smile for him. "Call it in Gallus, have them send an ambulance and a guard team. Have him transferred to the medical wing of the *carchar*. He's to be treated for his injury but he receives no visitors. We'll decide who gets to talk to him tomorrow."

Gallus did as she asked.

She looked down at Beynon. "You are under arrest for fraudulent entry and actual bodily harm. You have the right to remain silent, but you might want to consider how to exercise that in your own best interest."

He opened his mouth, but he changed his mind at the last second.

"We'll look after this twyll din until the cavalry arrives," Col offered.

Julia turned around to find Gallus had his phonecam in his hand.

"I need to take some shots of your injuries. Move into the light, filia mea."

Julia obliged and he hissed.

"It isn't just your throat. The tops of your arms are a mess too."

Julia looked down, to see clear hand-shaped bruises blooming. She shrugged. "He really didn't make any friends here. And I can't help but wonder what he would have considered to be sufficient pain to ensure my obedience."

A muffled scream drew her attention back to the tableau on the gravel, where Beynon's face had gone a strange shade of green, and there were slow tears leaking out from under his eyelids. Taking the rough with the smooth, she decided it was best not to notice.

"I guess I had better call Dai, and maybe Hook-Beak because I'd very much like to know how the irrumator on wristphone knew anything about Chingis, and his brother."

"Indeed." Gallus' voice steadied her. "Why don't I call Dai and set out what happened, then he can yell at me before you need to talk to him."

"Thank you. That would help so much. In the meantime I'll see if his nibs is still awake in Rome."

Hook-Beak was wide awake and firing on all cylinders. He was very interested to hear that there was a person of criminal leanings, with a working knowledge of the Mongol Empire, loose in Britannia.

After he had sworn a bit he calmed down enough to look at Julia. "What happened to your throat, puella?"

"His henchman."

"Where is this henchman now?" Hook-Beak's voice was deceptively mild.

"He's in custody. You just keep your beak out. Put your energies into finding out who would know the Manghud clan."

He showed her his teeth. "I shall certainly put out my feelers. And. Julia. In my experience henchmen are very good arena fodder."

Then he was gone.

Gallus gave her a worried look. "I can't raise Dai. Got Luned who said he went off somewhere with Bryn…"

Julia felt the gripe of worry, but automatically stiffened her spine. "I'm sure it's nothing. He's just out of wristphone range."

"Yes. That'll be it. I'm sure." Gallus sounded as if he was trying to convince himself too.

Julia sighed. "I know it's not like him, but I'm not going to find something else to worry about right now."

Gallus gave her a hug. "That's the spirit," he said, although there was definite concern in the back of his eyes.

"It's not so much 'the spirit' as me being too weary to try and work out what he is up to, and whether I should be worried or just plain annoyed."

"If you don't hear soon, I'll pop along to the *Mawddach* and ask around," Edbert said stoutly.

All of which was making Julia more nervous by the minute. She flapped her hands distractedly. "Stop pandering to me, you two. You're making me worry."

"We don't mean to," Gallus said, "it's just that…"

He was interrupted by a piping note from his wristphone. 'Olwen', he mouthed before answering. Whatever Olwen had to say it took a longish while and he listened intently. When he replied, his voice was warm with love

"I'll be home soon. I'm leaving now. Maybe you could make us a mug of cocoa."

Whatever Olwen replied made him smile. He bent to kiss Julia's cheek and was gone.

Edbert came to Julia's side. "You look about fit to drop. Can you make it to bed?"

"Yes. Of course I can. I'm all grown up now."

He smiled at her ramrod straight spine.

"Take the dogs with you and try not to worry about Llewellyn. The silly sod probably just got bored and went off on a jolly."

Julia privately thought that unlikely, but she kept her thought to herself, in the same way she would keep the sleepless night she foresaw to herself.

V

"I don't care if your wives will be hiring funeral actors if they don't hear from you," Vinculus said. "Right now I can't take the risk that anyone else might interfere in this operation. Each person who knows anything about it increases exponentially the risk of my target hearing or seeing something to unsettle him before I can get the evidence I need."

Dai, who was pretty sure Julia was more likely to be loading her guns and hunting for blood, looked at Vinculus in some exasperation. "I thought that the whole point was you didn't need evidence. You could just kill people who you thought looked shady."

"Divine Diocletian preserve me from fools!" Vinicus sounded incredulous. "Be glad that is not so or you two would be in trouble. It is not as though I am saying you may never see your women again, just not for a day or two at most."

"You clearly haven't met our wives," Bryn observed. "They might very well decide to come looking for us and that would get you all that attention you are trying to avoid."

"A risk I am willing to take." As he spoke Vinculus strode to the door. "Now I have wasted much too much time here. The vapour grenade was supposed to last no more than an hour. I was even wondering if it might have induced you both into coma, but then it was highly experimental."

Dai's anger flared.

"You risked us with some experiment?"

Vinculus shrugged. "It had been lab tested, this was its first use in the field. Now we are getting short of time so let's go."

Having very little choice, Dai followed, shooting a look at Bryn who shrugged his shoulders in response.

"What are you recruiting us to do?" Dai asked as they emerged from the bothy onto an empty hillside with a few sheep and some cottages visible dotting the landscape. Bryn's vehicle was parked up on a nearby track and Vinculus did not answer until he had opened the door and gestured Bryn to take the driving seat before getting in beside Dai as a passenger.

"You are going to be my eyes and ears. I have a drone watching somewhere for me at the moment but for all its capacity it is still not as good as an intelligent human. I am assuming you both qualify for that?"

Dai didn't bother to reply. He stared out of the window knowing how worried Julia would be and hoping against hope that whatever Vinculus required of them would not take very long at all.

Vinculus instructed Bryn to drive a short way to what looked like a local beauty spot carpark, where visitors on a day trip might pull over to admire the scenery. Another vehicle low and sleek was already parked up there. There was a view away to one side which overlooked the asclepieion and to another it gave a breathtaking vista of the land around finishing with the sea. Already twinkling lights were showing here and there in the landscape as dusk was beginning to deepen.

As soon as Bryn had parked, Vincilus was out of the vehicle and went over to the other one parked there, opened it and grabbed something from inside. Then he gestured to Dai and Bryn and the way down the slope into what appeared to be a small wood. They only had to walk a short distance to the edge of the fringe of trees. Beyond it the landscape looked not so very different from that which could be seen at the parking spot, a mix of wild moor and vaguely domesticated farm land, dotted with local cottages that looked almost quaint from this distance, but Dai knew well that close too they would be bleak and ill equipped. This part of Britannia, far from sight and mind of even the local administrative capital at Viriconium was an impoverished one. Vinculus gestured to the one decent looking property, a small villa nestled on the slope below them. It was of the same kind as Dai himself had been occupying with the children and clearly built to be a holiday let, offering all the comfort of home but on a much smaller scale. It's proximity to the asclepieion no doubt made it a popular place for those of wealth who might be either undergoing treatment themselves there or were wanting to be close to someone who was.

"Keep an eye on that place whilst I go and check on something. Don't move and stay put."

Then he strode back the way they had just come, leaving them alone. For a while they stood in silence looking at the house below and Dai wondered what they were supposed to be watching for. It was getting quite dark now and there were lights on inside, but all the windows were covered so it gave nothing away of what might be going on within.

"You think he is who he says he is?" Bryn asked, quietly. "I mean all that licensed to kill stuff?"

"I have a strong feeling he is. I've heard rumours. These are the kind of men that make even the Praetor nervous as they have no master except the Emperor himself and they will act on their own initiative if they feel the need."

"But he could have heard the same stories."

"He could," Dai agreed. "But then there is all that super-tech, the way he knocked us out, the ring…"

Bryn shook his head and sighed. "Yeah. That does kind of put the lid on the notion he is some kind of freaky fantasist, even if he comes over that way."

"Freaky fantasist?"

They hadn't heard Viniculus return and Dai gave a guilty start as he dropped a back pack on the ground between them and opened it.

"I…er…I…" Bryn stuttered.

"Here," Vinculus said thrusting an odd-looking wristphone at Dai and clipping it around his wrist. "This will keep you in touch with me. Don't try and take it off because you can't. You need to report anything just say 'Report' to activate it and then whatever you need to tell me. Got it?" Then before Dai could respond, "You watch this place and if you see anyone, you tell me and—"

He broke off and they all stared as the garage door began to lift. A moment later the familiar and gorgeous lines of the car Dai and Bryn had followed to Ynys Mon nosed its way out and started along the narrow road, picking up speed as it went.

Vinculus swore loudly.

"Stay here. Do what I said and remember if you let me down then you are betraying the Emperor himself." Then he turned and vanished at a run back towards the road.

The silence of the evening slipped around them and Dai found himself mentally counting to a hundred before daring to move.

"Well that was—" Dai started to speak but Bryn tapped his arm and he stopped, frowning. It was an old signal between the two of them calling for silence. Almost invisible, Bryn's gaze had moved to the wristphone Dai now wore and back, his expression urgent. For a moment Dai had no idea what that was supposed to mean and then he did. And Bryn was right. It stood to reason that the wristphone would be monitoring them, what they said and did, either in real time or logging it. "—very interesting," Dai finished and casually pulled the sleeve of his jacket over the offending article, just in case it had a visual feed as well.

Bryn winked and reached into his own jacket to bring out a flashlight, playing the narrow beam over the backpack Viniculus had left behind.

"Army ration packs, water, a set of binoculars…"

At the mention of food, Dai's stomach protested its day-long fast and he gratefully accepted the pack of nutrient bars Bryn held out.

"You eat first, bard, I'll keep an eye on the house."

Once they had both eaten, Bryn sighed heavily and made a lot of clearing up the wrappers, shoving them into a pocket. But when he pulled his hand out it was holding an old fashioned paper notepad and pen.

Dai grinned. He had teased Bryn enough in the past for his adherence to such low-tech methods, when they had been Investigator and Decanus back in Londinium, but this was not the first time it had proven valuable.

"So if that was Aemilius who left," Bryn asked as he scribbled on the pad, "then who are we supposed to be watching? His cook?"

"No idea. But if Dominus Viniculus says to stay and watch, I think we'd better do what he says."

"He is not someone I'd like to cross," Bryn agreed with feeling, then moved the pad and so Dai could see what he had written.

I can let Gwen and Julia know we are alright if I can get back to the all-wheel. If we don't they will have the whole province out looking for us!

"I wonder if he'll be gone long," Dai said and nodded towards what Bryn had written. "It's hard to see much."

Bryn got the message and nodded back.

"I have some binoculars with night vision back in the all-wheel. If our friend is not back soon I can go and fetch those."

"I'm not sure that is such a good idea as we were told to stay here and keep watch," Dai said quickly, his tone the complete opposite of the grin he gave Bryn.

"Well, Bard, we can't keep watch in the dark very well without something that lets us see what's going on down there. If we have to keep an eye on what the cook is up to we need those binoculars."

"I don't know…"

The wristphone beeped and Dai moved his cuff. There was a round and glowing orange eye now in the centre of the screen. Tentatively he touched it.

"You seen anything?" Vinculus' voice seemed to come from the eye.

"Uh… Not yet," Dai said.

"Stay put the pair of you. No wandering off."

"We were thinking of fetching some night vision binoc—"

"You are well equipped for a PI and a pen-pusher." There was a short silence and then some violent swearing, ending in: "Alright. One of you can get them."

The eye vanished and Dai covered the wristphone's screen again. So they had been right to be careful. Clearly they had been listened in on. He exchanged a look with Bryn.

"You go get the night-vision binos then," Dai said. "I'll keep an eye on the house for… well, whatever."

As Bryn slipped away into the trees Dai felt a little relief at the thought that at least Julia would not be left fretting.

Bryn returned a short time later with the promised binoculars and a thumbs up. He had found two heavy duty vigiles issue night sticks as well, which made Dai feel a bit better. At least they were not completely unarmed. Bryn had also thought to bring a couple of blankets from the all-wheel. In Britannia even the summer nights could still be cooler.

"Who's that, I wonder?" Bryn said as a lone vehicle could be seen it's lights threading through the countryside.

"Late night returner?"

"Very late. It's gone midnight."

Dai trained the nightvision binoculars on the vehicle but was little to see. "Looks like a hovercar. That's odd. Not many of them around this part of the world."

Bryns sharp breath made Dai lower the binoculars and look at the bigger picture again.

"Whoever it is they just turned into the lane that leads right to our target villa's portico," Bryn said. "You think we should tell our new boss?"

"We should, but if we can get a glimpse of who is in the thing…"

As it turned out and much to Dai's frustration they couldn't because as the vehicle approached the door of the garage opened and it slid inside.

"Whoever that was they are clearly at home there," he observed grimly and uncovered the wristphone. "Report. Someone just arrived at the house and pulled into the garage."

There was no reply and Dai sighed.

"Report. Some—"

The round orange eye glowed suddenly on the screen.

"I heard you the first time. It's likely the man who leased the villa. An administrator at the asclepieion, old patrician family hence happy to let the likes of Aemilus make use of the place. Now, I want you to—" He broke off. Then a few moments later. "Stay put. Instructions later."

'Later' was over two hours later and close to three in the morning. Nothing had stirred at the house, no one else had arrived. Dai had told Bryn to make use of the blankets and grab some sleep.

"Well that was a waste of time." Viniculus sounded angry, almost sullen, although his voice was controlled and quiet as ever. "The driver was not my man at all, just his hired help who had no knowledge of anything except being told to drive north like the Furies were after him. He couldn't even say for sure where Aemilius is, or even if he was ever at that house. I'm not far from the Caledonian border and won't be back with you for at least another four hours. You keep watching the place. If you get so much as a glimpse of anyone let me know. Got that?"

Dai said he had and then settled back wondering what they were supposed to do if they did see Aemilius. With just a night-stick apiece he and Bryn were not much of a match for a top level Mongolian infiltrator.

Bryn touched his arm and indicated he should rest. Dai handed over the nightvision binoculars and gratefully curled himself into the blankets.

"I hope you're not falling asleep on the job, Llewellyn."

The wrist phone apparently monitored his vital signs as well.

Sighing Dai sat up and stared into the darkness.

***

Julia gave up on sleep well before dawn, and she slid from her tumbled sheets with a heavy heart. Walking to the window, she looked out on a foggy night, but one that promised another scorching day when the mists burned away, she sighed,

"Where are you Dai bach? I so hope you aren't in trouble."

She was saved from further introspection by the insistent buzzing of her wrist unit. A single glance told her it wasn't her errant spouse. It was Hook-Beak, which meant it would have to be answered. She turned the bedroom light on with some reluctance and thumbed the screen.

"Don't you ever sleep?" She could hear the scrapes of worry and pain sharpening her voice but was too tired to really care.

"Not much. And nor do you by the looks of things. Neck paining you?"

"A bit. But I've mislaid Dai."

Hook-Beak frowned. "It's that idiot of a magistratus. I told her she had no need to put him on gardening leave. But she's a member of the Imperial faction so she's long on procedure and short on imagination. If he doesn't turn up today I'll send you a few bored praetorians. They'll soon shake him loose."

Julia managed not to let him see how that though horrified her. "You didn't call me before *gallus cantet* to discuss my bruises or my errant spouse."

Hook-Beak offered her his best crocodile smile. "No indeed. I am big with information. I have finally got a handle on the body hunters. It seems there has been a spate of high-value jewel thefts. From *Noricum* to *Narbonensis*, a series of daring cat-burglar robberies has seen something like ten million sesterces worth of baubles has been liberated from the wealthy and useless. The insurance people are enjoying multiple heart attacks and the praemium is suitably humongous. Anyway, nobody knew where to look next. Until you got a run of jewel thefts. Which is why the praecipuum ponebaturs are circling around you like flies. I've let it be known that I will be irritated if they don't treat you with respect. Other than that, I have the details of the thefts. Where do you want me to send them?"

"Angie Ffrydd please. It's her case."

"You might want to rethink that, Julia. The name that is being bandied about is Cluntius. Tiberius Cluntius Callidus"

"Cluntius?"

"Yes. As in Ancilla Cluntius Blandia, who is a guest of your Magistratus."

"I don't see her as a cat burglar. She's barely able to walk".

"Was I you, I'd be checking up on that disability."

Julia sighed. "I might just do that. But you can still send the paperwork to Angie."

He looked as if he might be going to argue, but something about the set of her chin must have given him pause. He nodded once.

"Try not worry about your stupid spouse; he'll turn up."

He cut the connection and Julia stared blindly at the blank screen for about ten seconds. Then she squared her shoulders and contacted her immediate boss.

Domina Agrippina wasn't best pleased to be awoken early in the morning, but when she understood what Julia was saying she sat bolt upright in bed with a wrinkle of concentration marking her high, white forehead.

"Are you telling me my cousin is a common thief?"

"No. I'm telling you she is suspected, and that the people who suspect her have very few scruples."

"Very well. I will talk to her."

"Please do. It would be very embarrassing if the praecipuum ponebaturs were to make an arrest in your household."

Pina looked grim. "It would. Thank you for the heads up."

Julia couldn't think of anything else to say and she was about to end the call when Pina held up a hand.

"There's also the son to consider. Tiberius, she called him. The one I was persuaded to recommend for an administrator's job at the asklepieion on Ynys Mon. Shall I contact him?"

Julia almost kicked herself. Of course, Pina had mentioned the son before, why hadn't she thought of that?

"No. Better not. I'll see to him."

"Thank you again, Julia."

Pina's face disappeared, and Julia mentally reviewed the conversation. Something about it left her feeling like a cat who had been rubbed backwards, but she couldn't put her finger on precisely what. She sighed. Had it not been for a polite tap on the bedroom door, she might have indulged herself in a few tears, however, when Edbert poked his head into the room she had herself well in hand.

"Gwen Cartivel is in the kitchen. Wants a few words."

"She's very early. Send her up. And will you wake someone and order ientaculum in the garden please?"

He nodded, whistled up the dogs who had kept Julia company through what had felt like a very long night, and went away on silent feet. Julia carried on looking at the murky sky, only turning when she heard Gwen's familiar footsteps. She raised a smile for her friend, who slipped into the room and shut the door behind her.

Gwen opened her mouth to speak, then she must have caught sight of Julia's throat, because she hurried forwards with her hands outstretched.

"Edbert said you were a bit bruised, but I'd call this rather more than a bit bruised."

"I haven't looked recently."

Julia moved to where her mirrored dressing table stood. Her throat was a mess, black and red and purple, with four fingers and a thumb clearly delineated. She lifted the thin sleeves of her nightgown to study the rings of bruises about her upper arms, and shrugged.

"Beynon was very brave when he thought he had his hands on a defenceless woman—irrumator changed his tune when I shot him."

Gwen managed a tight grin. "Sit down and let me look at your neck."

Julia sat and let herself be fussed over.

"Are you able to swallow properly?"

"I think so. I think it's more dramatic than dangerous."

Gwen carefully explored her neck with gentle fingers. She smiled.

"It's not going to offer you any permanent problems, but I'm sure it's painful now."

"Not if I don't think about it."

Gwen shook her head fondly. "You are just stubborn enough for that to be true. But your injuries didn't bring me here.

I got a message from Bryn. It was sent last night but I didn't get it until I woke up this morning."

"You did?" Julia sat up straight, bruises forgotten. "What did he have to say?"

"Basically, he and Dai are okay. He can't say what they are about but if I don't hear again inside twenty-four hours will I please send out the cavalry."

Julia had a think. "Nobody can raise Dai, so how did Bryn contact you?"

Gwen fished in her pocket and took out a scruffy plastic tablet. "We have a pair of these. A retirement gift from some boys in Londinium. They have been heavily modified. The range is impressive. But they can only send and receive texts."

Julia grinned. "And it looks like an eReader not a communicator. That's clever. Can Bryn's be tracked?"

Gwen fiddled and a map came up. "It's not very accurate, Bryn says to a hectare, but they are showing up as being somewhere in the region of the asclepieion on Ynys Mon."

Julia sighed. "Everything seems to be pointing us towards Ynys Mon. But why?"

Gwen put her hand on Julia's cheek. "Perhaps the universe wants you at Ynys Mon."

Feeling completely unable to deal with Druidic fatalism Julia was groping around in her head for something to say when her wristphone burbled again. It was Pina.

"Julia. Sorry to disturb you. But Ancilla is in a fearful funk about her gods-bedamned son. I told her you would speak to him, but she came over all maternal and tried to call him herself. Only his wristphone isn't connecting, and now she's behaving like a ewe who has lost her lamb."

Julia sighed. "Tell her I'll make sure to contact him."

Pina smiled. "Just so you are sure you're speaking to the right man…"

A picture flashed up on screen. It was a face Julia had seen only the previous night. Sneering and threatening. She kept her own face carefully bland, although inside she was angrier than she had been for a very long time.

"I'll remember his face," she said calmly before Pina broke the connection.

Gwen was a shrewd woman and she immediately understood that something had bitten Julia's buttocks.

"What has so disturbed you my friend?"

"Last night I saw Beynon's boss on a wristphone. Making threats. I made a few promises of my own for when I caught up with him. Which was more than a bit optimistic as I didn't know who he was at the time. But now I do know. And I'll see him at the gates of hades."

Gwen smiled at Julia's vehemence, but then she sobered. "I'd better leave you then, I don't want to get in the way."

Julia put out a hand. It helped to have someone as calm and solid as Gwen around when things were so turbulent. "No. Please. Stay and eat with me. I've a fair bit to organise before I go hunting at Ynys Mon."

VI

The sky began to pale and not for the first time in his career as a vigiles, Dai got to watch the glory of the dawn unfolding in the skies above and over the landscape below. Bryn yawned and stretched then leant back against his chosen tree.

"Might be time for breakfast," he suggested, "if you can face more of those bars."

They admired the dawn as they munched the tasteless rations. Then Dai's attention was caught by something moving on the road. He lifted the binoculars and saw it was a local taxi service, it's logo stamped boldly on the side.

He followed its progress from sheer boredom, but that slowly changed as he realised the route it was taking.

"Looks like someone is leaving early," he observed, then remembering he was supposed to not know he was broadcasting all the time, said the word report and repeated himself. "There's a taxi pulling up at the house. Do secret agents travel by taxi?"

"Not if they have a car to hand," Viniculus said, as if that was obvious. "Though they might if..."

"Not much we can do from here to stop him leaving if it is for Aemilius," Dai pointed out.

"I'm doubting the man was even there," Vinculus said, "I think this has all been an elaborate ruse and by now he is in some ship he picked up off the coast and heading home to *Karakorum* with his ill-gotten gains which will not doubt do more harm. I just would love to know how he figured we were onto him."

"So we can give up and go home?" Dai asked hopefully.

"No you stay there and keep watch until I get back. There is always an outside chance I'm wrong."

Which was, Dai thought, quite an admission for a man like Viniculus to make.

In the end they were unable to see who it was that got into the taxi as the vehicle pulled up by the side door and the low sun meant that it was impossible to see through the windows with the binoculars as it pulled away.

Dai duly reported all this and got a dismissive reply from Vinculus.

"Side door? Then that'll be a servant going somewhere."

"Unless they know the house is being watched?" Bryn suggested.

"Or realised that if it was then it would have to be from these trees and that side of the house would be the one—"

"Yes, yes. It's a servant. Now shut up and keep watching."

Soon after the garage opened and the car that had arrived the night before slid out. Dai reported the fact and got no reply.

"Think it's broken?" Bryn asked him.

Dai shrugged.

"Could be, or out of range of a satellite." Or could be the cunnus of a special agent just couldn't be bothered to answer. It was very hard to know.

A couple of minutes later the back gate of the villa that faced them, opened and a man came out dressed as if he planned to go for a day's hike, like any tourist. Which would have been little problem except he was heading straight towards them at a brisk pace.

"Report. We have a hiker incoming." Dai hissed into the watch.

That was met by silence.

"Typical," Bryn said softly, "when you don't need it the thing works and when you do it fails. "What do we do, bard?"

Dai thought quickly. He had a feeling that the answer from Vinicus would be hide in the woods and avoid the hiker.

"I'm wondering who he is and what's going on at the house. Might be nice to have a casual chat with our tourist. So I think I might be out for a walk having parked up at the beauty spot."

"Bit early for a walk, isn't it?"

"I'm with my dog, but he's run off."

"Right. So I'm surplus to requirements," Bryn decided and scooped the blankets, backpack and other traces of their stay into an armful and headed for the nearest undergrowth.

The hiker had changed direction very slightly to follow a path and Dai made his way quickly through the trees until the hiker was a short way ahead of him.

"Lovely morning," he said cheerfully.

The effect was not what he had expected.

The hiker spun around and there was a gun in his hand. A pistol with what looked like a silencer on the barrel.

Dai froze. Keeping his hands very much in sight and away from his body.

"Uhh! I'm sorry. I didn't mean to—"

"Who are you?" the hiker snarled. "What are you doing here?"

"I'm just out walking my dog," Dai said and waved a hand vaguely towards the road. "I parked up at the beauty spot and—"

"Dog?"

"Yes, small terrier. Called Bryn. Have you seen him?"

There was a slight look of doubt now in the hiker's face.

"Turn around or I'll—"

The blow from behind was hard enough to stun the man and Dai stepped quickly in to grab his wrist and take the weapon as he dropped like a felled tree. Bryn lowered his nightstick and glared at Dai.

"So you called your dog 'Bryn'?"

Dai laughed. "It was the first name that came to me seeing your face over his shoulder. I can't think why that was."

"So what do we do with him? Take him back to the villa?"

Dai shook his head.

"We've no idea who else might be there, or how many."

Then he lifted his wrist towards his mouth. "Report. Report." Silence. Dai thought back to what he had seen when studying the landscape.

"There looked to be a bothy or some other kind of place on the edge of the next field and it has a track to it I'm willing to bet goes up to the road. Let's take him there and," he reached down and unstrapped the wrist phone pressing the unconscious hiker's index finger against the screen to bring it to life, "we'll call for support."

***

By dint of a great deal of hustle and bustle two all-wheels left the Villa Papaverus just as the sun poked its pink nose over the horizon. They headed north for Ynys Mon and, even allowing for dipping in and out of visibility-clogging patches of thick mist, they weren't hanging about.

Julia sat in the front of the first vehicle, with Edbert driving. Gallus shared the back seat with four wolfhounds and Angie Ffrydd. Angie had reported that the Broanon's had given her the name Cluntius in their eagerness to distance themselves from whatever was going on. And they had shared the information that Caeso Maol had been arranging to smuggle the jewels out of the province but had apparently either become greedy and decided to keep some or careless and lost some, which was what had led to his demise and the desperate searching of his home and warehouses.

The second vehicle carried six of the biggest and most trusted vigiles, three from Julia's section and three from Dai's. Everyone felt that something big was about to happen and it was almost possible to taste the readiness in the air.

The drive might have been nightmarish had not Julia had implicit faith in Edbert's ability to wrestle any vehicle into submission. She was forced to admire Angie's nerve as the girl leaned back against the seat cushion, idly chatting with Gallus and stroking Huginn's wiry fur.

They were nearing the bridge to Ynys Mon when Gallus spoke up.

"Do we know where my *filius in lege* is precisely?"

"No. I've got about a square mile. But the dogs will find him."

"They will indeed." Edbert's unfeasibly deep voice was as reassuring as ever.

Once across the water, Edbert abated his dangerous pace and the two vehicles adopted a more sedate speed. As they made a left turn to head towards the asclepieion, Julia glanced in the other direction along a short driveway which was made grand by a decorative arch where it left the road and finished in expensive wrought iron gates. These, as she recalled, protected the entrance to an extremely exclusive country club, with its pools and golf course, and restaurants, and private airfield. She saw a man with a briefcase climb out of a tacsi and pass the saluting gate guard without a glance. She briefly wondered how such arrogance came to be in a common-looking local cab; it seemed to be striking a bum note somehow.

Before she had time to chase that thought down, though, her wristphone burbled. It was an unfamiliar call sign and she might normally have let it go to voicemail but something in her gut was telling her to answer. As she lifted her wrist, Angie leaned over from the back seat and wrapped a gauzy scarf around her throat.

"You might want to keep the damage hidden."

"Good thinking." Julia touched the screen and was rewarded by the sight of Dai's face. Her relief was so intense that for a moment she could not speak. Then she drew a breath and words came.

"Lovely boy. Where in Hades have you been?"

"Long story short. Me and Bryn were forcibly recruited by someone calling himself Vinculus who says he's an Imperial Special Agent. We were set to watch a house. Which we have been doing. We caught some character trying to leave who drew a gun on us. Now we can't reach our spymaster and we have a prisoner neither of us is currently in a position to arrest. So I stole the prisoner's wristphone and called you—basically to say I'm okay, I love you. And please send help."

Julia found herself able to laugh. "Are you on Ynys Môn?"

"Yes."

"Me too. Edbert's already locked on to your signal. He says fifteen minutes. I love you too…"

She blew a kiss. Ended the call. And hung on for dear life.

Twelve minutes later the two all-wheels halted at the end of the badly maintained track leading to the outbuilding where Dai and Bryn were currently keeping hold of the man they had caught trying to leave the district so secretively. If he was an innocent citizen, Julia was prepared to apologise nicely and send him on his way—but instinct was telling her they had one of the bad guys in hand at last.

She gave a few brisk orders then headed inside. Gallus and Angie walked a pace behind her, and she knew both would have hands on their weapons.

As she put a hand on the door she heard a hectoring voice.

"You can't hold me. I'm a Roman citizen and I'll see you face the arena for this impertinence."

Julia couldn't hear what Dai replied, for the sound of the blood pounding in her ears. She knew that voice and its propensity for making threats. It was, she thought, time to see if the man had the testicles to back up his arrogance. Somehow she doubted it.

Pushing the door open, she strode into the room. She nodded pleasantly to Dai and Bryn before turning her attention to the man who was handcuffed to a chair.

"Well, well, well. If it isn't Beynon's boss."

She put a hand behind her and snapped her fingers. "Shotgun," she barked.

"Immediately Submagistratus." Gallus sounded very much as if he had snapped a salute, but as Julia knew him exceedingly well she could detect a thread of unholy amusement under the professional woodenness.

Julia looked closely at the face of the man who had professed himself willing to sell her whereabouts to her enemies. She said nothing, and a bead of perspiration gathered at his hairline. Behind her, Dai cleared his throat as if he was about to speak, but he said nothing—which Julia tended to put down to either Bryn or Angie's influence,

The sound of firm footsteps heralded Gallus' return. He came to her side and presented the shotgun she had ordered.

"Loaded and cocked, domina."

Then he stood back.

Julia let the silence stretch out and watched without a shred of feeling as the man in front of her began to disintegrate. When she judged him to be right on the edge she lifted the gun.

"Which leg shall I do first? Do you have a preference?"

He whimpered and Julia allowed herself a smirk.

"Permission to speak, domina?"

It was Gallus in his best harsh praetorian tones, and Julia wondered what he was up to, but she nodded.

"Official guidelines suggest the left knee. Seems less likely to provoke a loss of consciousness."

"Very good." Julia altered her aim slightly and Tiberius Cluntius Callidus screamed.

"Somebody stop this madwoman. She can't just go round kneecapping innocent Roman citizens."

Dai seemed to have caught on because he replied quite calmly. "No. She can't, but I fail to see what that has to do with you."

"I think he thinks being Roman gives him an edge," Angie said with equal calmness. "I wonder how long it will be before he realises that the Submagistratus wouldn't care if he was the offspring of Caesar's sister and the Praetor of Rome, or the bastard child of a Camelopard and a river alligator. He threatened her and she told him what would happen when she caught up with him."

"And here I am."

Dai coughed gently.

"Was there something?" Julia managed not to laugh at the genuine panic she could sense coming from her over-gentlemanly spouse.

"I was just thinking that our friend here really doesn't have many options."

"Indeed he doesn't," Julia purred. "Perhaps you would like to lay them out for him while I decide which of his kneecaps goes first."

"Well. He could keep his mouth shut and get his knees shot to smithereens. Then you'd ship him back to Rome, where I think threatening the Praetor's foster sister would earn him a turn in the arena. Or. He could sing like my mam's pet canary and hope to earn himself a clean death."

Callidus folded his lips together and closed his eyes.

"Of course there is a third option," Angie said brightly.

"And that is?" Gallus picked up the ball with consummate ease.

"Londinium and crucifixion. It's all the fashion now. I wonder how long he'd last with two shot knees hanging on a cross on an island in the river. They say some folks actually live for days…"

Tiberius fainted.

Bryn grinned at the assembled company before picking up a bucket of water and throwing it over the unconscious man.

He lifted his head.

"What do you want to know?"

Julia hefted the shotgun.

"All you know. And you'd better pray it's enough."

It was like the breaching of a dam and Julia was heartily glad of the ever-efficient Angie, who produced a recorder from her pocket and captured the torrent of words that spewed from Tiberius' lips.

Bryn looked at him in barely concealed irritation. "Well," he said to nobody in particular, "we do seem to have laid hands on a proper little one-man crimewave."

Julia sort of stopped listening and turned to look at Dai. Which was the first time he actually saw the wreck of her throat. He was at her side in two strides.

"Who? How?"

Then he could say no more sweeping her into his arms and holding her as if she was made of spun glass.

She looked up into his face. "No time to talk now. I'm fine. I really am. As soon as I knew you were okay…"

Gallus put a hand on Dai's shoulder. "Before you start to feel sorry for that irrumator there, you should understand that Julia was hurt on his orders."

Angie looked up from her recording device and showed her teeth. "He's admitted to being up to his bollocks in the jewel thefts, told us who murdered our bent merchant, and now he's giving us chapter and verse about a mongol spy and some experimental drugs being developed at the asklepieion. He really has been a busy boy."

Dai stood straighter. "What's he say about the mongol spy, Angie?"

"Just that he was working for one and met the man yesterday to hand over the entire research portfolio from the asklepieion. No name though."

"I think I might have a name," Dai said and fiddled with the phone. "Show him this."

Julia saw the screen and had a lightbulb moment. "Who's he?"

"The man me and Bryn have been hunting for."

"What, Mamercinus Aemilius Lepidus?"

"That's him," Angie confirmed.

Julia grinned and punched Dai lightly on his biceps.

"I think we just might have him." Even to her own ears her voice sounded like tearing silk.

"What? How can we have him? We don't know where he is."

"But we do know where he is. Or at least we know where he was about a half an hour ago."

"What?"

"I saw a man getting out of a tacsi outside the country club gates. This man."

"But won't he be long gone?"

Julia felt a feral grin spread across her lips. "I don't think so. Visibility is okay down here, but up on the ridge, where the country club is, it's like pea soup. That place is exclusively socially exclusive but then as the joint submagistratae of the area, so are we, so they should let us on the premises without us needing to raise a hue and cry and alert our spy. So I'm sure Gallus and Angie can manage here if you're up for a little hunting trip."

His answering smile was every bit as vicious as her own. "Why yes, my lovely wife, a hunting trip sounds as if it would be extremely profitable."

Dai lifted his wrist with an odd looking wristphone attached.

"But there's this. Our special agent was using it to keep tabs on me and get me to report in. He snapped it on like a handcuff and it doesn't seem to come off again. And although it seems to have been pretty dead for a while now, it could spring back to life at any moment."

It was Gallus who answered quietly. "I just happened to have a way to deal with that about my person." He took a pair of bolt cutters from the tool pouch he habitually wore and cut the strap with a snap.

Julia didn't dare look at Dai's face, but from the unholy amusement in Bryn's eyes he was having a bit of trouble maintaining proper stoicism.

Angie rescued him by grinning at Gallus. "Once a praetorian, always a praetorian. Ready for anything."

Gallus laughed. "Of course."

Julia risked a look at Dai, who was now openly grinning at his vitricus. "We'll leave you to deal if the owner turns up. But be careful he's tricksy and wholly amoral."

"Bit like myself then. If he comes here he's toast. Now go."

They needed no second telling and pausing only so Dai could equip himself with a spare vigiles wristphone, they ran to where Edbert leaned on an all-wheel pretending boredom.

"No time to explain. You and the dogs are under Gallus' command until I say otherwise."

He was wise enough not to argue, simply whistling the dogs and heading inside the farmhouse.

"Okay Dai boy. Drive like your backside is on fire. I've a couple of calls to make."

She called Rome, and was fortunate enough to get one of Hook-Beak's more intelligent functionaries. She was put straight through.

"Hook-Beak. No time for niceties. Keep quiet and listen. We have one of the Emperors mopper-uppers crawling about here. He's after a mongol spy. But what makes it interesting is the spy's name: he's one Mamercinus Aemilius Lepidus."

"Aemilius?"

"Yes." Julia knew she had just handed Hook-Beak a weapon to use against his most powerful enemies, and she could see the second when the denaruis dropped and he started calculating.

"Thanks Julia. I owe you. And did you find your errant spouse?"

Julia turned the screen of her wristphone so that Hook-Beak could see Dai, who was driving with fierce concentration.

"You look busy."

"We are. Hunting."

"Well. Good hunting Julia mia."

"You too."

Hook-Beak's smile was that of a satisfied predator.

Julia ended the call, and contacted Pina.

"Ah. Julia. I was wondering where you might be. It's all a bit odd here. Ancilla has disappeared, presumably, with a half dozen praecipuum ponebaturs in her wake. Before her pursuers shot off, one of them said there is now direct evidence connecting her with at least one robbery in Noricum. Her son sold off some of the haul. Now I'm unsure what to do."

"Do nothing. The son is in custody and he's arena fodder. You just need to look imperial, unapproachable and a little confused."

Pina actually laughed. "I'll do that. Annia says I'm good at that expression. As to the rest, I neither need nor want to know, do I?"

"You don't. But there is something practical you can do. Aemilia Aemilius Secunda is a very young woman and about to be left alone and friendless in a strange place."

"I'm guessing that how and why is among the things I don't want to know. I won't ask, but I will help her. Annia and I will make sure she's all right."

"Good. It was a bit of a worry."

Julia ended that call, just as the gates of the country club loomed out of the gloom.

VII

The Viridi Iugera Domus was so exclusive even before you could approach the gates you had to drive under an arch with the inevitable eagle that declared it to be a sub aquila property to its extreme boundaries. Seeing that set Dai's teeth on edge, but getting through the gates was easier than he had expected.

He had been prepared to be as bullishly obnoxious as required, but the man on the gate was a recently retired vigiles from Viriconium who recognised both Dai and Julia and was delighted to allow them in.

"We were in the area after a long night and thought we'd treat ourselves to ientaculum in the last civilised outpost of the Empire," Dai said by way of explanation.

The gate guard nodded understanding and wrote that as the reason for their admittance as visitors.

"If you know what you would like to eat, dominus, I can order it up for you from here," he added helpfully.

Dai glanced at Julia who entered into the spirit of the thing by quickly reeling off the kind of menu any fat patrician might expect to break his fast on, enough to feed a family of four at least. Then with a mischievous twinkle in her eye added: "Oh and I'll have just a freshly squeezed orange juice for myself."

The helpful gate guard noted it all down as she spoke, before telling Dai the best place to park and then opening the gates.

So it was in laughter rather than grimness they arrived at the quietly grand villa, which meant they were smiling as Dai felt the reassuring weight of a pistol in its shoulder holster pressed against his tunic and under his jacket as he helped Julia from the vehicle and then reached in to grab a nerve whip and clip that to his belt too.

Beneath the folds of her stola, thrown on over the workaday tunic and trews beneath, he knew Julia was similarly well armed and met the sparkle in her eyes with a wink, before turning to face the sober doorman with the gravitas expected of a high ranking Roman official.

As they were admitted to the building and shown through to the *triclinium*, Dai knew a familiar frisson, tingling from the soles of his feet to lift the hair on his scalp. He did not doubt for a moment that the man they were here to arrest was probably more personally dangerous than any other they had confronted and would have no compunction about who or what he damaged to ensure he could get away.

But Dai was also sure that the man purporting to be Aemilius was unlikely to do anything to betray himself until he was one hundred percent sure that the game was up, because to do so would turn his orderly withdrawal into a risky rout. From having met him, Dai was also pretty confident that Aemilius was going to be a man of the same order of magnitude in self-assurance as Viniculus and likely to try and bluff his way through, rather than reach for a weapon or a hostage. But even so, Dai was glad, as they entered the almost completely empty room, that this was a time of day that the Viridi Iugera was at its quietest.

This palace was designed to meet the demands of the elite of Britannia and even those who were of Romano-British—or even pure British—stock wanted the trappings of Rome, so there were no tables such as one might find in a British based establishment only the discreet arrangement of groups of couches, set between screens and potted plants to give some privacy to each group of people eating.

As they were shown in, it was obvious only two other triclinia were occupied. One by a couple who seemed very much involved with each other and oblivious to their surroundings. Dai had them pegged as newlyweds doing a grand provincial tour before settling back into married life in Rome. The other was occupied by a single man who seemed to glance at his wristphone a lot.

Dai felt a lift of his spirits and turned to the man escorting them who was waiting for them to indicate where they might like to sit.

"I see someone I know," he said and gestured to the man sitting on his own. "Mamercinus Aemilius Lepidus. Perhaps you would be kind enough to ask if he minds if Domina Julia and I join him?"

The flunky obliged and Aemilius looked over and studied them from beneath hooded eyes for a moment and then nodded, adding something more to the flunky who shook his head and seemed to be apologising.

Not waiting to be escorted, Dai took Julia's arm and led her over to the couches, nodding amicably to Aemilius as he settled her on one with due chivalry before taking the last couch himself.

The flunky murmured something about the meal the dominus had ordered being on its way and withdrew.

"Submagistratus," Aemilius said, "to what do I owe this pleasure? And is this a—" he hesitated just long enough to make the implication he wished, "a lady friend?"

Julia gave a feral grin at that.

"I'm also a submagistratus," she said firmly and Aemilius nodded as if he had not just been appallingly rude.

Dai choked back his anger at what he was sure had to be a deliberate insult.

"This is my wife, Submagistratus Domina Julia Llewllyn."

Aemilius lifted a brow.

"You have abandoned your name, domina, in the British fashion. Have you also abandoned your attachment to other aspects of Roman culture?"

Dai bit down on his tongue knowing Julia was more than capable of handling such probes.

"Not all," she said sweetly, "only those that I find restrictive. It is good to have the best of two worlds, I find."

"How is your daughter?" Dai said quickly before Aemilius could speak again. "Is she here with you?"

"Aemilia Secunda?" Aemilius frowned. "No. She is at home. I am having to make a business trip and was supposed to be flying from here a couple of hours ago but this wretched mist has all the planes grounded. So until that lifts, which I am assured should be within the next hour or so, I am forced to wait. What brings you and your wife here?"

"Work," Dai said, attentive for any reaction. "We have come to Ynys Mons in pursuit of a criminal."

Aemilius merely nodded.

"I suppose you must keep some odd hours in your job at times," he observed. "Did you get your man? Or," he nodded at Julia as if what he was adding was in honour of her presence, "or woman?"

"Not yet," Julia said sweetly, "but we are getting close."

The arrival of food put paid to any further conversation and Dai made great play of feeding Julia the choicest morsels from his own plate. Aemilius watched her bruised throat with an expression that made Dai want to grind the other man's face into the icy marble of the floor. Arresting him was going to be a real pleasure—even if it did need to be done with the sort of discretion that would preclude handing out the physical punishment Dai felt was merited.

Outside, the sun made a brief appearance, and Aemilius grunted.

"It looks as if the fog is lifting," Julia said brightly, and the brittle gaiety of her voice made Dai wince. Somebody, he thought, was in for it. He might even have felt a bit of compunction, if the man in front of them was not so eminently dislikeable.

Food finished, Julia drifted out onto the wide balcony which overlooked the airfield. It felt to Dai as if she exerted some sort of subliminal pull as both he and Aemilius followed on her heels. The mist was lifting rapidly and by any reckoning, it wouldn't be long before a plane could take off. It was beginning to look like now or never, and Dai was reaching for his weapon when his wristphone burbled. It was Bryn's call sign, so instead he excused himself and nipped back into the room to take the call.

"Look out, bard. That slimy twll din, Vinculus is on his way. He's furious his toy stopped working and has been swearing he will take it out on someone called Cue or something that sounds like that."

"That's what happens if you rely too much on the tech," Dai said.

"Preaching to the choir, bard, preaching to the choir. Anyway, Viniculus took off like he'd a jetpack tied to his backside. Said he's damned if you are going to get the credit for his hard work."

"*His* hard work?"

"Yes. Apparently he intends to claim that he unmasked the spy. And caught Tiberius. But Gallus is talking to someone in Rome right now to stop that little caper. If you can lay hands on Aemilius."

"I'm about to."

Bryn chuckled. "Vinculus is not a happy boy. Gallus made him give over our wrist units and threatened to arrest him for using an untried sedative on innocent citizens. It was like watching an irresistible force smash right into an immovable object. He's disturbingly impressive when he's annoyed, isn't he?"

"He's disturbingly impressive however you cut him…"

Dai turned to look back out onto the balcony. To find Aemilius and Julia gone.

"Oh merda…Gotta go Bryn."

As he spoke he was outside and looking about in some worry. Then his heart leaped into his throat as he saw Aemilius and Julia walking down the broad staircase that led towards the grass. There were stairs down from the balcony, but these were now shut off by a security gate, no doubt activated by Aemilius.

If you looked idly they seemed to be in friendly conversation, but Dai was pretty sure Julia was being held against her will. He could tell from the tension in her body and could see one of Aemilius' hands, the one carrying a brown leather document case, the other was out of sight but Dai was willing to bet there was a gun in it pointing at Julia.

There was also a small aeroplane taxi-ing across to the departures area.

This was rapidly turning into a *trychineb* and he needed to move fast. The balcony was too high to risk a drop so without a second's thought he started to run. It was something he did well and did fast, trained in it from his earliest youth. He was lucky, in that his trainers made little noise on the smooth floor and there was no one else about to get in his way.

He burst out of the last door to arrive on a broad stone-flagged patio from which one could view the airfield. He could see the plane had come closer and Aemilius seemed to be urging Julia to move more quickly. She turned her face up to his and although Dai couldn't see her expression he saw Aemilius bare his teeth in a rictus that bore little relationship to a smile.

Dai knew even with his own impressive turn of speed he wouldn't reach them before his quarry was onto the grass, and he didn't want to be chasing them across the airfield, figuring that would put Julia in even more danger than she was already. Just as he was beginning to wonder if he would be justified in shooting Aemilius without challenging him first, he had a brainwave.

The grassed pathway leading to the plane ran briefly along the side of the building almost directly below where he was. There was a wall on the edge of the patio. It was a drop of about ten feet or so, but he was confident of his own athletic ability and the ground looked fairly soft. He stopped running and jumped up onto the wall. Regulating his breathing, he took the minute or so before Aemilius and Julia were directly below him to calm himself and make ready. Casting out a prayer to any god that might be watching he jumped, aiming for Aemilius' broad back. Julia must somehow have caught the movement from the corner of her eye for she turned to face her captor and spat what must have been a vile insult because he raised an arm to backhand her, just as Dai landed almost astride his back.

Years of running and youthful acrobatics had taught Dai to fall, but even so it was a jarring landing as Aemilius crumpled under him. It should perhaps have been enough to bring the man to the ground, but Aemilius was good and had started to move aside so they both fell awkwardly.

Dai had endured more than enough of spies, and criminally inclined Romans with all their entitlements and arrogance. He got to his feet, ignoring the protest from his knees and rolled Aemilius over before grabbing the Roman by the neck of his tunic and ploughing a fist into his stomach. Aemilius blocked it and drove a knee up into Dai's gut but then something snapped inside Dai's head and a red mist, denser than the rolling fog, rolled through his consciousness, driving away everything but the need to destroy this man who threatened Julia. He had an awareness of his own fists beating and pummelling with a force that seemed beyond his own strength, then Julia's voice broke through the red mist.

"Stand down now, lovely boy. We want to leave something for the arena."

It took him a few deep breaths to recover but he found himself grinning at her as she pulled the handcuffs from her belt. Normally his uncontrolled anger left him feeling shame, but this time it was different. This time it had been Julia's life on the line and nothing else mattered.

They had Aemilius cuffed hand and foot before airport security ambled their way.

As he recovered a little, Julia made a quick call on her wristphone and, by the savagery of her smile, boded no good to the prisoner.

The uniformed guard, whose badge proclaimed him 'Head of Security', stopped about six feet away and saluted. "Submagistratus," he said respectfully, "we were coming over to help but you seemed to have it in hand."

Dai was recovering, but now he let himself notice his knees and fists were protesting a bit, so he was glad when Julia answered for him.

"He did indeed have it in hand. This man's a Mongol spy."

It was very obvious the head of security here was praetorian trained because he didn't even blink.

"Oh well, in that case we'd better stop his aeroplane hadn't we?"

He spoke quickly into a small radio pinned to his chest and another uniformed security guard took out the plane's tyres with a shotgun. The plane yawed a bit before coming to a halt.

Dai's wristphone burbled again. This time it was Gallus.

"Do you have your hands on the spy *fy mab*?"

"I do."

"You're a good lad." The pride in his *llys-tad*'s voice warmed him, reminding him of the way his da had sometimes spoken so many years ago.

122

***

Julia looked at her beloved husband and thought he was going to be very sore come tomorrow morning, but for now he was riding on adrenaline and barely-banked anger.

Aemilius stirred and groaned and she bent to his ear. "If I was you I'd keep quietly still, in case my boy, there, remembers you again. Before your busy brain sends you the wrong idea, I won't let him kill you. And nor will I let the emperor's dog have you and offer you a quick death. Oh no. There's a helicopter on its way from Londinium right now and it's full of praetorians. They will be escorting you to Rome."

Julia looked into his eyes, watching for the moment the truth of his fate dawned on him. When it did she switched her attention back to Dai and airport security.

"You wouldn't happen to have somewhere we can stash the consignment until his transportation arrives, would you? The copter left Londinium half an hour ago, so it should be here in about thirty."

"We've a sturdy cell in the base of the tower. I'll get some guys to carry him."

Another terse command into his radio and a couple of thickset men trotted out of a door at the base of the air traffic control tower. They hefted Aemilius between them.

"Nobody gets near him without my say-so," Julia said quietly.

The men dropped Aemilius and saluted.

She smiled at the security chief.

"The helicopter is crewed by a crack praetorian extraction squad. On orders of the Praetor himself. He doesn't forget those who help him."

The chief's chest swelled with pride and he, too, saluted Julia.

She put a hand on Dai's arm.

"I know it's early, but I could do with a big glass of wine."

He smiled down at her. "Me too."

By the time they got back into the domus, the manager himself was front and centre, bowing obsequiously.

"We'd like a table out on the balcony," Julia said in her most patrician voice, "and a bottle of something vaguely decent to drink. I don't suppose you have any Llewellyn Red?"

The manager was forced to admit that they did not, offering a grand cru Mamertinum from Sicilia as a substitute. Julia inclined her head and he scuttled off.

Ten minutes later she and Dai were ensconced on the balcony in a pair of comfortable chairs drinking a truly noble wine and nibbling on stuffed olives, sun dried tomatoes and sharp, salty cheese.

As soon as the last server departed, Dai looked down at her with laughing devils in his eyes.

"You, my love, are priceless."

"I'm only behaving how they would expect me to."

"Precisely, but I could never carry it off."

"No. You are too much of a gentleman."

He shrugged. "Maybe. But now I have some questions."

"Fire away."

"Firstly I need to know who had you by the throat."

"Bedwyr's baby brother, Beynon. On the orders of that piece of ordure you and Bryn laid hands on. I was to be bullied into not investigating Tiberius' private crime wave."

"But?"

"But I had my little antique Derringer in my pocket. Shot him through the leg."

"Where is he now?" Dai sounded truly dangerous.

"He's on his way to Londinium. Didero was talking about the arena." She felt Dai relax. "You said questions."

"Oh yes. How did you manage to conjure up a helicopter full of praetorians?"

"I didn't. Hook-Beak got to thinking that he didn't want our spy to be quietly assassinated, so he had Didero assemble a squad and send them this way. Felicitously as it turned out."

She watched Dai's face as he worked his way through that one. "Factional infighting?"

"Slightly more than that. If people get wind of the praetorian guard getting their hands on spies, spying suddenly seems a less attractive career."

Dai nodded. "Yes. It would at that."

Julia smiled at him and they raised their glasses to each other.

A small disturbance heralded the arrival of the Imperial spy. He was flanked by large security guards and blustering for all he was worth. Julia put a hand on Dai's lips.

"Allow me, adored one."

He grinned and sat back with the air of a man about to be well entertained.

Vinculus pointed a shaking finger at Dai.

"You are a dead man walking," he snarled.

"Don't be any stupider than you can help." Julia's voice had quite the bite of a whip and Vinculus turned, mouth opening then something he saw in Julia's face made him close it again.

She looked him up and down, from his dishevelled head to the toes of his boots, and saw the second when he realised himself outgunned. He inclined his head, but still glared at Dai.

Julia wasn't about to let that go. "You," she said coolly, "are already in enough trouble without further antagonising the husband of the Praetor's foster sister. Right now, my brother doesn't know your name or your face. Would you have me enlighten him?"

Vinculus' lips tightened.

"Perhaps not, domina."

"Perhaps not indeed." She smiled her sweetest smile. "And as long as you forget about us, I will forget about you when he asks me. Now, can we offer you a lift back to Rome? We are expecting a helicopter full of praetorian guardsmen."

Vinculus couldn't hide his disquiet and Julia had to grin. He started to back away, and security bracketed him once more. Julia didn't doubt for a moment that he'd slip their grip and be vanished back into his shadows and long gone before the praetorians arrived.

Once Vinculus had been eased from the room, Julia crossed to Dai and hugged him. "As soon as Hook-Beak's boys arrive, we can probably go home. We could even swing by the Mawddach and collect the children on the way."

His smile was like a blessing.

"Indeed we could, beloved. Home and family. Somehow that sounds such a wonderful idea," and he stooped his head to kiss her softly.

Glossary of Latin and Other Terms

Please note these are not always accurate translations, they are how these terms are used in Dai and Julia's world.

achubwyr - rescuers

Anno Diocletiani - Year of Diocletian. The calendar dates from the birth of Diocletian, the reforming emperor who established the foundations of a new empire

arglwyddes - lady

asclepieion - healing spa, hospital

atrium - and open air space in the middle of a building, used as an outside room

Augustus - the month of August

bach(m.)/*fach*(f) - literally small/little, term of endearment, 'dearie' may be closest

Britannia - we would call it Britian

carchar - prison

caupona - an inn or hotel

cerbyd hyfryd - gorgeous vehicle

Cinio - meal eaten at the end of the working day

cornu - war trumpet used for issuing orders

Demetae and Cornovii - Wales and several English Midland counties including Shropshire

domin-a/us - Ma'am/Sir. Used to superiors both in rank and social status

dyn bach - little man

filia mea - my daughter

filius in lege - son in law

fui draconum - jackal

futator - fucker

fy mab - my son

gallus cantet - cock crow

gentes maiores - families that claim descent from the early rulers of Rome

gwillion - ghost or bogeyman

ientaculum - breakfast

irrumator - cock sucker

Italia - we would call it Italy

Karakorum - capital of the *Mongol Empire*

lectus - dining couch

llys-tad - stepfather

Londinium - we would call it London

Mawddach - area around the Mawddach estuary

Magistratus - senior official with legal jurisdiction over an area

mea culpa - 'through my fault', my bad

medic-a/us - doctor

merch - girl

merda - shit

mingo - piss

moecha - literally 'adulteress' metaphorically: 'slut' or 'tart'

Mongol Empire - enemy of Roman Empire controls most points east of Europe

Narbonensis - we would call it Provence

Noricum - we would call it Austria

parva - literally small, term of endearment

Penllwyn - we would call it Capel Bangor

popina - cafe or cafeteria

prandium - brunch or lunch

Praetor - an extremely high-ranking official in Rome

praecipuum ponebatur - bounty hunter

puella - girl

spado - literally 'eunuch', metaphorically 'stupid fool'

stola - female formal wear, a pleated dress

sub aquila - literally 'under the eagle'. An eagle above the entrance of any building means it is Citizen access only - aside for those who might work there of course

submagistratus - a more junior official with legal jurisdiction over an area, under the authority of a Magistratus

taberna - pub/bar

toga - male formal wear

Traeth Abermaw - we would call it Barmouth Beach

tributum officium - tax office

triclinium - dining room, with groups of three couches set around small serving tables.

trychineb - disaster

twll din - asshole

Vigiles - Police. In Dai and Julia's world the police are a sub-branch of the military

Villa Papaverus - Poppy House. Dai and Julia's home.

Viriconium - we would call it Wroxeter. The area capital of *Demetae and Cornovii*

Viridi Iugera Domus - Green Acres House

vitricus - stepfather

Ynys Mon - or the Isle of Anglesey

If you enjoyed reading this Dai and Julia adventure, please leave a review and be sure to sign up to <u>Working Title Blogspot</u> where you can learn more about their upcoming stories and keep in touch with the authors:

<u>Jane Jago</u>, a genre-hopping maniac, who could no more stop writing than she could stop breathing. Her current obsession is dragons. But who knows what next week will bring. For the full list of her published writings see https://author.to/janejago

<u>E.M. Swift-Hook</u>, author of '<u>Fortune's Fools</u>' series of books, whose favourite quote on writing is one Robert Heinlein put into the mouth of Lazarus Long: '*Writing is not necessarily something to be ashamed of, but do it in private and wash your hands afterwards.*' Having tried a number of different careers, before settling in the North-East of England with family, three dogs, cats and a small flock of rescued chickens, she now spends a lot of time in private and has very clean hands.

Printed in Great Britain
by Amazon